Moose Island:
Maine Murder Mysteries

William Graham

© May 2020 William Graham

All Rights Reserved

Other Works by William Graham

Poetry
Vox Publica
Terra Incognita
The Places You Can Go: Poems for Children
Amoricon and Other Poems
Smugglers' Notch
The Sweetest Swing: Baseball Poems
Interlude
Work: Labor Poems
Gathered Leaves: Selected Poems
A Good Place to Wake Up: Vermont Poems
The Love Poet of Vermont
The Storm Subsides: 50 Poems of Passion and Protest
Mountain Springs: Haiku from Vermont
Lengthening Shadows
Wolf Moon

Young Adult Fiction
Danny Boyle and the Underland
Danny Boyle and the Ghosts of Ireland
The Boy with the Golden Arm
Volcano Island
Kid Island
Olivia Turner's Amazing Amazon Adventure
Maddie the Dog

Fiction
Fire and Ice
Newfoundland Sagas
The Red Planet Trilogy: Three Novellas
The Red Planet President: A Novella
The Last Inning: A Baseball Novella
Greenfields: A Novella
Smoking Mountain: A Novella
Martian Darkness: Four Detective Ace Sloan Mysteries
Atacama Red: A Pablo Nelson Mystery
The Green Mountains Murders: A Detective Sophie Junot Novel
The Devil You Know: A Detective Sophie Junot Novel
Gilded Crimes; A Detective Sophie Junot Novel
Under Currents: A Detective Sophie Junot Novel
Bluff City

Travel
Seven Continents: A Travel Memoir
Border Crossings: Travel Essays and Poems

Biography

Poet, novelist and travel writer William Graham holds a BA and MA in English and a MS in Communication from Northwestern University in Evanston, Illinois. He lives in Stowe, Vermont.

PART 1: INCOGNITO

1

From their home on the highest point of Moose Island, Samantha and Phil Nugent could not see the Maine coastline ten miles to the west. The island, so named by early settlers because its shape resembled the long snout of a moose, was enveloped by a thick fog that had lingered for two days. On clear days, they could see in the distance the harbor of the small coastal town of Stillwater Cove, which had a few basic essentials for residents and visitors: a gas station, a small grocery store, a post office, and a vintage bred-and-breakfast. But today, Samantha and Phil might have been on another planet that was a billion miles from Earth. The couple felt that isolated.

But moving to the island was of their own doing. One year ago, on the summer solstice, they moved into their three-bedroom shingled cottage after having fled from their vintage townhouse in Boston. Phil had discovered while searching online a posting that the general store on Moose Island was for sale. He hated his job as a corporate lawyer and had always wanted to move to Maine. For eighteen years he and his brother Mike had spent the summer with his grandparents at their home near Acadia National Park.

Even though he had no practical business or retail experience, his sense of angst about his job, mixed with his nostalgia for the Maine coast, caused him to make a monumental life decision and purchase the business after one visit to the island. He convinced Samantha, his wife of seventeen years, that the move would be good for them and their two children: fifteen-year-old Rufus and eleven-year-old Maggie. He convinced Samantha that she could maintain her graphic design business as easily from Moose Island as she could from Boston. Skeptical at first, Samantha reluctantly agreed to the move, with the caveat that if, after two years, things did not work out, they would return to Boston.

"I'll make it work," Phil pronounced optimistically.

The first year had been a difficult transition, especially for their kids, who had to adjust to attending a small school that had only fifteen other children, ranging from kindergarten age to two high school seniors. Weather permitting, two teachers from the mainland, one for grade school and one for high school, came to the island for just three days during the week for in-person classes. The rest of the children's education was conducted virtually, if the island's spotty internet service permitted it.

Phil had to learn quickly how to order essential supplies for the island's residents and for the tourists who visited. The store carried everything from hand tools to toilet paper to T-shirts to groceries to fishing gear. Everything on the island came in on one of the ferries that serviced the island three times a day. Phil's life revolved around hearing the loud horn that announced the next ferry had docked. After the first year, he was pleased that he had managed to turn a modest profit. But his income was nowhere near what he had earned doing legal work. The family's balance sheet had taken a severe hit over the past twelve months.

Samantha's graphic design business, however, had continued to flourish from her home office on the island. She was now the primary bread winner, as she served corporate clients throughout New England.

Moose Island

On this foggy June day, Rufus climbed on one of the island's rocky cliffs that plunged over two-hundred feet to the roiling ocean below. Because of the fog, Rufus could only hear the pounding waves below him. He carefully scrambled over the slippery rocks. He had his iPhone with him, as he planned to make a video and upload it to his YouTube channel where he chronicled his teenage life on a rocky island that had just one-hundred-twenty-five permanent residents. As he panned his phone camera from the pine trees behind him to the cliffs in front, he heard a scream in the distance. Keeping the camera recording, he gingerly walked to the cliff's edge. The breeze had shifted, allowing a momentary break in the fog bank near the cliffs. He zoomed in. He then saw a body splayed on the rocks two-hundred feet below. Frozen, he did not at first know what to do. Then he sprinted back home through the pine forest to show his mother what he had recorded.

2

Julien Pelletier looked out of his bedroom window to observe a sea of white fog. He groaned and burrowed back under the covers. The chill felt more akin to what it should be in October, not June. He rolled his body closer to his wife of thirty-five years: Julia. He looked at his phone. It was still just seven o'clock in the morning. He didn't need to open his combination souvenir and sandwich shop called High Tide until nine o'clock.

A retired detective from the Boston Police Department, Julien moved to Moose Island five years ago after putting in thirty years with the force, first as a patrol officer and then working his way up to become a detective. His wife,

Moose Island

Julia, a native Mainer from Southwest Harbor, worked as a waitress at a seafood restaurant in Boston after graduating with a degree in French literature from Boston College. Julien met Julia at the restaurant when he was investigating an armed robbery there. A year later they were married. Julia was a stay-at-home mother who reared their two daughters, who now both worked in Boston, one as a strategic consultant and the other as a dentist. They were proud parents, hoping to become grandparents one of these days. Although neither daughter was in a rush to exchange their careers for motherhood.

An avid runner, Julien had remained lean as he aged and his hair became gray. He liked to take a run through the island's trails before opening up the store. On foggy mornings, however, his motivation sagged.

"Aren't you going for a run?" Julia asked. Raised by a father who was a lobsterman and a mother who delivered mail in a boat to small inhabited islands off the rugged Maine coast, Julia had a ruddy, wind-whipped face that was framed by flowing white hair that she refused to dye. She claimed that she wanted to both look and think her age. "My hair color shows my hard-won wisdom," she said. "I'm not thirty, and I don't want to be."

7

"I suppose I should," Julien said. "If I stop, I'll get in the habit of doing so. And then I'll regret it."

"Do you think the ferries will run today?"

"The fog is supposed to lift by mid-morning. So, I expect will have a pretty good crowd of day trippers from the mainland."

Julien put on his running gear and headed out into the fog-shrouded trails. Moving to Moose Island was originally his wife's idea. After living in Boston for more than thirty years, she was ready to move back to Maine to be closer to her aging parents. When their kids were younger, they had rented a cottage for several summer holidays on Moose Island; they loved the tranquility. Over time, Julien came to appreciate the serenity of the place. On the island, he didn't have to deal with murderers, drug dealers, and rapists. His blood pressure dropped immediately after stepping off of the ferry.

For the first year on the island, Julien and Julia relaxed in their new home that overlooked the sea on the south end of the ten-mile-long island. But they both became bored, and were getting on each other's nerves. When an opportunity arose to buy High Tide from the previous owner who decided to retire to the big city of Portland, Maine, they jumped at the chance. Julien handled the souvenirs (post cards and T-shirts) while Julia made soup and sandwiches that were served from eleven in the morning until three in the afternoon only. Although they both wanted to work and meet the tourists, they didn't want to be consumed by the business. So, they limited the shop's hours from nine o'clock to three-thirty. Between the modest earnings from their business and Julien's police pension, they lived comfortably.

As Julien's run progressed, he limbered up and began to enjoy the island's remote natural sublimity. He inhaled the aroma of the pines and the sea. He leapt expertly over the rocks that studded the trails that snaked through the forest. He ran in a five-mile loop to the center of the island and then back along the cliffs near his house. As he headed home, he encountered his neighbor Dave Carr, who owned a sea kayak business. Julien stopped to catch his breath and to chat. It was the neighborly thing to do on Moose Island.

"What do you think, Dave? How does the sea look today?"

"Once the fog burns off, we should have good weather and calm seas. I have ten customers booked for a tour this afternoon," Dave said, with a barely visible eastern European accent.

"Good for you," Julien said. A year after moving to Moose Island, Julien and Julia met Dave and his wife Natalie. Dave explained that he was a retired professor of Russian from Williams College. Natalie had taught math there. But they were avid outdoors people who spent every summer break in Maine, they explained. After retiring two years ago, they opened the kayak business, which Natalie ran while Dave led the tours.

Julien said his goodbyes to Dave and decided to walk the remaining quarter mile back to his house. As he rounded a bend on the trail, a young boy whom he recognized as Rufus Nugent came flying by, nearly knocking him over. By the time Julien yelled a greeting, Rufus had disappeared.

"How was your run?" Julia asked.

"About the same. Although I was nearly involved in a hit-and-run with Rufus. It was if his pants were on fire," Julien said. "Strange. Anyway, time for a shower and then it's back to the coal mines for both of us."

"Yes, our life is so tough here," Julia said, laughing.

3

Nadine McAfee, a detective in the central district of Maine's Major Crimes Unit (MCU), pleaded through a locked door for a man to release his ex-wife and infant child. Two days earlier the man had killed his ex-wife's mother out of revenge and spite; he blamed her for her daughter's decision to divorce him. For two days, Nadine had been searching for the ex-husband, who had disappeared into the woods after the murder of his ex-mother-in-law. Then a report came in about a disturbance and gunshots being fired in a small house in the hamlet of Cobb, Maine.

Two other officers joined Nadine. They covered the back of the house while Nadine tried to start a dialogue with the man from the front porch. Nervous and still unsure of herself since she had just been promoted to detective less than a year ago, Nadine tried to calm the situation by telling the man to think about his young daughter, who had her entire life ahead of her. For a few minutes, the man engaged in a tense conversation with her. Then there was an eerie silence inside the house.

Nadine heard the woman crying and pleading for her ex-husband to release her. During the time she had been standing on the porch, Nadine noticed that the front door of the house looked flimsy. It had a vertical crack running up the side. Even though she knew it was against protocol, she stepped back from the door, lowered her shoulder, and then slammed into the door with her full body weight and momentum. The door splintered and swung open. Startled, the man fired a shot at Nadine. The round struck her in her bullet-proof vest. But she kept rushing toward the man, tackling him and holding him down. Then the two other officers flew in: one to help subdue the man and the other to escort the woman and her daughter out of the house.

After the gunman had been taken away, Nadine remove her vest. A large bruise had begun to form under her right shoulder, which had begun to throb with pain.

"You were lucky," one of the officers said.

"I knew my rugby playing skills would come in handy one day," Nadine joked.

***

Nadine had played women's rugby in a club while she was an undergraduate at the University of Maine in Orono. She was a psychology major. But upon graduating, she joined the police academy because of her lifelong goal to serve the public. For the past twenty years, since she was ten years old, Nadine had lived in Maine. After Nadine's parents had both been killed in the 9/11 attacks in New York City, her maternal grandmother Martha, who lived in Waterville, had volunteered to take her in.

Eighty years old and becoming less mobile by the year, Martha now depended on Nadine to watch over her. For three years, Nadine had lived in her own house with her now ex-husband Duke Granger. She had met Duke four years earlier. He had owned a small sporting goods store at the time, and he was an avid outdoorsman. Their mutual love of the outdoors at first cemented their compatibility. But over time, as they took longer and longer camping trips into the most remote regions of Maine, Duke's survivalist paranoia reared its head. He tried to persuade Nadine to quit her job with the state police and live with him in a yurt. She could grow food in a garden while he hunted for fresh meat, or fished in the pristine rivers. He explained that he didn't want to be under the thumb of the government, whose sole purpose was to infringe on his freedom. Nadine couldn't tolerate the regular sermons from Duke. She eventually told him to move to the woods if he wanted, but that she would not be joining him. Duke eventually did sell his business and headed for the proverbial hills to live out a life of secluded bliss.

After the divorce had been finalized, Martha's health began to deteriorate, which compelled Nadine to move in with her. But Duke continued to haunt Nadine's life from time to time. Nadine would receive reports from colleagues on the state police force that Duke had been involved in minor scrapes with the locals. Apparently, he regularly ignored signs that warned of trespassing on private property. And he dismissed the need for hunting or fishing licenses. Over multiple occasions, Nadine pulled strings to either get the charges dropped or to pay his fines. Martha just shook her head at Nadine when she learned of these tales.

"Why do you continue to help him?"

"I did love him once. He's basically harmless. Just a little overzealous at times."

"Never make your decisions on what once was," Martha advised. "He's a grown man; leave him be. He made his own bed, or whatever he sleeps in up there; let him lie in it."

Martha's old house with its tilted and worn wooden floors felt comfortable to Nadine. Even though frail, Martha loved to bake, especially apple and blueberry pies. The house always smelled like a bakery.

"How does your shoulder feel, dear?" Martha asked.

"Sore, but healing," Nadine said.

"The world is going crazy."

"You're not going to tell me once again how things were better in your day."

"Not better, but different. More civil, I would say."

"We have to live in the world as it is, Grandma," Nadine said. "Isn't that what you're always telling me?"

"Yes. But we don't have to like it."

"No, we don't. You're right about that," Nadine said, smiling.

***

"You ever been to Moose Island?" said Captain Roy Davies, to whom Nadine reported.

"No."

Davies was a thirty-year veteran of the Major Crimes Unit. His short-cropped, military-style hair had gone white. His uniform was pressed sharply. His badge glistened. He had been pressed by his superiors to elevate more women to the detective ranks. Nadine had been a standout officer. She was tough and thorough. Davies felt confident that she could handle anything, which for him, was saying a lot, for he had climbed the professional ladder in a male-dominated force.

"Well, welcome to your next case," Davies said. "All we know is that the body of a young woman, possibly a teenager, was found dead on the rocks at the bottom of a cliff. The Coast Guard has recovered the body and taken it temporarily to a funeral home in Stillwater Cove. I know that normally a body is not supposed to be moved, but the recovery team was afraid the body would be washed out to sea."

"Who found the body?"

"Apparently a boy on the island heard a woman scream. He has a video and audio recording on his phone."

"Are you having the body sent to the medical examiner in Augusta? I'll need to know the exact cause of death."

"The body is being picked up this afternoon," Davies said. "You'll need to be on the ferry dock at nine o'clock tomorrow morning to catch the first boat to the island. I've arranged for you to stay at the Albatross Inn while you begin your investigation."

"I've heard the community on these Maine islands is quite close knit," Nadine said. "Somebody must know something."

"At this point, we don't know if the woman was a local or a visitor. Even though the island has a small year-round population, it welcomes thousands of tourists from May until October."

"There was no identification found with the body? No one has reported a woman missing?"

"The Coast Guard team said they found no ID to identify the woman."

"Thanks for assigning me such an easy case."

"You're one of our rising stars. Here's your chance to really prove it."

4

Nadine's en-suite room at the Albatross Inn was comfortable, but a bit too quaint for her taste. With its walls covered with photos and watercolor paintings of birds and sailboats, the room reeked the worst of Maine kitsch. Tourists may find such ambience likable, but Nadine knew that real Mainers were rugged and independent, not delicate or whimsical.

She had packed enough clothes for two nights. Although she wasn't sure if she needed to stay that long. But, then again, she would stay as long as she felt that the investigation into the unknown woman's death yielded clues. As she unpacked her duffel bag, she discovered that her grandmother had surreptitiously packed for her a bag full of oatmeal cookies. Nadine was glad that none of her colleagues saw this; they would undoubtedly have mocked her. Nadine smiled and placed the cookies on the nightstand near her bed.

The fog from the day before had lifted. Moose Island was bathed in a warm sun under sumptuous blue skies. She had two interviews to conduct today: one with Rufus Nugent and the other with Julien Pelletier.

But before she started the interviews, she pulled out her paper map of the island that the owner of the inn had provided her. She wanted to see where the body had been discovered. Nadine began walking on a trail that meandered through the island's scattered homes until she entered a pine forest. The trail rose and then fell for about one mile until it opened onto the rocky precipice, below which the Atlantic crashed into large boulders. This is where the woman's body had been found.

Nadine surveyed the area. There were no footprints on the rocks. She found no evidence that the woman or her possible assailant had dropped anything. Could the woman have come to the island with the intent of killing herself?

Nadine thought that this cliff would be the perfect place for a desperately depressed on confused woman to take her own life.

In looking at the map of the island, Nadine realized that every trail converged at this spectacular lookout point. The woman, or her killer, could have arrived here from anyplace on the island. And, given the fact that there was a dense fog on the day she died, the chance of any of the islanders seeing or hearing anything was diminished. Nadine realized that she would need to walk on every trail on the island in a search for clues.

Satisfied, however, that there was no evidence to be found on this rocky outcropping, Nadine returned to the village and walked to the house where Rufus lived.

"Mr. and Mrs. Nugent, I'm Detective McAfee," she said. "I called earlier."

"Yes, please come in," Samantha said. "This is my husband Phil. Please take a seat. I'll go get Rufus."

Nadine took a seat in the small but inviting living room with polished wood floors and expansive views of the ocean. She could see what attracted people to the island, although in winter the charm combined with the gnawing isolation would test anyone's mental reserves.

"Hi, Rufus. I'm investigating the death of the woman who was found the rocks. I understand that you were making a video for your YouTube channel. Is that right?"

"Yes," Rufus mumbled, obviously nervous.

"Speak up, dear," Samantha said.

"That's all right. I heard him clearly," Nadine said, trying to put Rufus at ease. "Can you show it to me?"

Rufus handed Nadine his phone. She watched a video that showed little more than a fog-shrouded cliff. Then, faintly in the background, she heard a woman saying "No, no, no" and then there was silence. The video then showed a break in the fog through which a body could be seen briefly far below on the rocks. The time stamp read ten minutes after seven in the morning.

"Please send me this video, Rufus. I'll need it as evidence," she said. "Tell me, Rufus, did you see anyone on the cliff when you made this video?"

"Nobody. I was there alone. Or at least I thought I was."

"No one on the island has reported a teenage female of approximately seventeen years of age missing. Did you happen to notice a girl on the island that you didn't recognize, maybe someone who was acting strangely?"

"No, sorry. There are a lot of tourists who come here just for the day. I don't even notice them anymore. They usually stay closer to the harbor where the shops are, like Dad's."

"How about you, Mr. Nugent? Did you happen to see anything at your store that seemed out of the ordinary in the past few days?"

"I can't say that I did," Phil said. "Other than Rufus's video, we don't have much to offer you, unfortunately. And I haven't heard any rumors about the young girl either. On this island, rumors spread fast among the locals. But I've heard nothing."

"Well, if you hear that one of your neighbors suddenly remembered something or saw or heard anything, please call me," Nadine said, leaving her business card. "Now I'm off to talk with Julien Pelletier. I understand that he was out for a run on the day you were videotaping. Is that right, Rufus?"

"Yeah. I nearly ran into him on my way back home," Rufus said.

"You and Julien have something in common," Samantha said.

"Really? What's that?"

"He was a detective in Boston for thirty years. He might be a real help to you."

"I guess I'll find out," Nadine said, although she was concerned that Pelletier might want to stretch his old investigative muscles and get in her way.

Nadine walked to Julien's store, where he was busy unpacking a fresh inventory of T-shirts and hoodies.

"Hi, you must be Julien Pelletier. I'm Detective Nadine McAfee."

"It's a pleasure to meet you. You've got an interesting case on your hands."

"I just learned that you used to be a detective."

"That's right. But I sell T-shirts and hoodies now. Can I interest you in one to memorialize your stay on Moose Island?" Julien said, laughing.

"Maybe later. For now, tell me if you saw or heard anything when you were out for your run that morning."

"Other than almost colliding with the Nugent boy, I saw nothing. The fog was very thick."

"But you went for a run anyway?"

"I could run these trails blindfolded. I'm a bit of an obsessive when it comes to running. Tell me, has the girl been identified?"

"No, not yet," Nadine said, as she mentally braced herself for the onslaught of questions that this ex-detective was about to pepper her with. He couldn't help himself, she thought. But since he had eyes and ears on the island, she decided to indulge him.

"She's obviously not a local. She would have been reported missing. Do you know the cause of death yet?" he said.

"Not definitively. But it was likely major trauma caused from the plunge to the rocks. I'm waiting for the conclusive report from the medical examiner."

"You should scan the missing persons database to see how many matches with females her age pop up."

"I'll make sure I do that," Nadine said. "I'll be on the island for two days. If you can think of anything that might help me, give me a call."

"I'll be sure to do that. I know that these cases can keep you up at night."

Nadine returned to her hotel, grabbed one of her grandmother's oatmeal cookies, and then reclined on her bed that featured a thick quilted blanket. She heard the horn announcing the arrival of the next ferry. Soon, the island would be covered with people seeking a moment's bucolic respite from a hectic and cruel world.

After two days on the island, Nadine had uncovered no leads as to what happened to the woman or even who she was. She returned to Waterville, where Martha had told her that Duke had been arrested for breaking in to a summer home and stealing food.

"An officer came by to tell you, but I told him that you were away working on a case," Martha said.

"So much for being a fucking survivalist," Nadine said. "I'm going to let him work his own way out of this latest mess."

"Good for you," Martha said.

5

While at her home in Waterville, Nadine learned that the woman had died of strangulation and was dead before she had hit the rocks. Moreover, according to the medical examiner, the woman had been raped. This knowledge heightened the sense of urgency to solve the case.

Nadine informed Captain Davies of the results of the autopsy.

"Do we know who the woman is?"

"Not yet," Nadine said. "I need to return to the island and find out how she arrived there, where she was staying, and for how long she had been on the island."

"Return to the island and stay as long as you need to solve the case. With the tourist season about to ramp up as we get closer to July, we don't want to incite panic about a killer."

"I'm focused on finding a killer, not about the public relations implications," Nadine snapped back.

Nadine told Martha that she would be returning to the island for an unknown period of time.

"If you need groceries, I've already spoken to Sandra next door. She will drive you to the store while I'm away. If something urgent arises, call me. I'll be on the next ferry back to the mainland," Nadine said.

"I'll be fine," Martha assured her.

With extra clothes and provisions packed, Nadine drove to the port in Stillwater Cove, where she caught the early afternoon ferry to Moose Island. The day was humid and a light drizzle obscured the island as the ferry pulled into the dock. As Nadine disembarked along with dozens of tourists, she waved to Phil Nugent, who had arrived in an ATV with a wagon attached to transport inventory back to his store.

"Do you have any leads on the case?" Phil asked.

"I've returned to continue the investigation. That's all I can tell you right now," Nadine said.

"Do you need any help with your bags?"

"No, thanks. I'll be fine. I know the way."

Quickly exiting from the scrum of people at the dock, Nadine walked through the rain to the Albatross Inn, where the owner Mitzi Fairhaven greeted her.

"I was able to reserve for you the same room you had before," Mitzi said.

"Thanks. I don't know how long I might be here, however," Nadine said, removing her rain jacket.

"You stay as long as you need to. It was terrible about that girl's death. But I was afraid something like this would happen on the island one day."

"Why? What do you mean?"

"In the summers, there are lots of pretty young girls on the island. Some of them are college girls who work at the big Sea Breeze hotel. You know, the Victorian monstrosity on the hill right above the dock. My place is much cozier, as you know yourself. Anyway, for years I've heard that the man who runs the electrical power station on the island sometimes harassed the girls."

"Harassed how?"

"Telling them how beautiful they were. Or sometimes showing up at the beach while they were in their bikinis and just staring at them. He claimed he never did anything wrong. Plus, the islanders know that he's a mechanical genius, so they tolerate his eccentricities."

"And you think he could have killed the young girl that was found by the cliffs?"

"Oh, I wouldn't want to accuse George of that. That's his name: George Pennyman. I'm just telling you what I heard. There are lots of rumors floating in the air on Moose Island."

"Thanks for information," Nadine said. As she walked up the stairs to her room, Nadine wondered how much stock she should put into Mitzi's gossip. Before doing anything, she wanted to get background information on George Pennyman. A few minutes surfing through public information on the internet and police databases revealed that Pennyman had been accused of harassing his first wife before their divorce became final. His ex-wife had secured a restraining order against him four years ago while he worked for a power company in Bangor. Shortly thereafter, Pennyman left Bangor and took over management of the island's small, but critical, generating plant.

Nadine located the power plant in a clearing in the center of the island: a squat, square building constructed of cement blocks with a nearby high-voltage power array.

Nadine also noticed workmen installing several large solar panels. She asked one of the workers where Pennyman was.

"Are you George Pennyman?" Nadine said. Standing before her was a tall man with an imposing head like an anvil. He wore a T-shirt even though it was overcast and cool, with a breeze blowing in from the east off of the Atlantic.

"Yes. And you are?"

"Detective Nadine McAfee from the Major Crimes Unit. I'm investigating the death of the young woman here in the island. Do you know this woman?" Nadine then showed him a photo of the dead woman that was sent to her by the medical examiner.

"Never saw her in my life. I heard about what happened, of course," Pennyman said.

"I've heard that you like to follow young women around the island."

"Kind of hard to avoid it. I travel all over the island working on the electrical grid. In the summer, the island swarms with people. Some of them happen to be attractive women."

"You do a lot of electrical work at the sandy beach on the east end, George? You know, where young women are sunbathing."

"That's a nasty question."

"What's your answer?"

"So, yes, I sometimes talk to these girls. There's no crime in that. I'm a single guy. I try my luck. Maybe I come on too strong at times. People are so sensitive these days."

"Welcome to the twenty-first century," Nadine said. "Where were you three days ago around seven in the morning?"

"Right here. I'm usually in by seven."

"Can anyone verify that?"

"Yeah, the guys over there working on the solar panels. Ask them. I'm trying to be environmentally conscious. I want to supplement the island's four, sixty-five-kilowatt, diesel-fired microturbines. Welcome to the twenty-first century, Detective McAfee," Pennyman said sarcastically. "And, by the way, this is a small island. Don't believe all of the rumors."

Chastened and slightly embarrassed by her conversation with Pennyman, Nadine headed back to the Albatross Inn. She wondered if the upcoming days would be filled with finger-pointing, suspicions, and rumors rather than hard leads. She encountered Julien Pelletier on the trail. He was heading to the dock to pick up groceries.

"Detective McAfee, I heard you had returned to the island."

"Call me Nadine. Word spreads fast round here."

"You've figured that out," Julien laughed. "You've spoken to George, I take it?"

"How did you know that?"

"Like I said. A small island. Since George arrived, some of the older islanders have cast a suspicious eye on him. He has a record. But I'm sure you know that. He's not a killer or a rapist."

"How do you know these details?"

"I have my contacts in law enforcement, even here in Maine. I want to know what happens on this island," Julien said.

"In regard to George, I agree with you. He has an alibi," Nadine said.

"Like I told you before. This is going to be a tough case. Anyway, I'll see you around."

Later that afternoon, Nadine retreated from her room and sat in a rocking chair on the covered porch of the Albatross Inn. The sun had finally made an appearance.

The sea glimmered like a diamond. If she didn't have a job to do, she thought to herself that she could live here. This place can seduce people, she mused.

6

On the far northwest side of Moose Island, where the land is too rocky and undulating to build modern homes, Rufus Nugent found one day while wandering the island a small, abandoned cottage, whose roof had partially collapsed. Hidden by a thick grove of trees and far off from any walking path, the structure offered Rufus and his teenage friends a secret and secluded place to gather on the island. Having a place to gather, drink beer, and smoke joints was a great luxury for the small cadre of teenage boys on the island.

"I think an artist used to live in this building a long time ago," Rufus told his friends Henry and Bryant, who were sixteen and seventeen years old respectively. "There are some easels and some old paint brushes in the corner."

"You're not going to video this place for your blog, are you?" Henry said, sipping from a beer bottle.

"No way," Rufus said. "This is our place. Hey, Bryant, did you get the weed?"

"Right here," he said.

"I got some sweet new videos that I want to show you guys. Look what I found while filming above Puffin Beach the other day."

The trio peered into the screen of Rufus's phone. They watched as a group of young women nude sunbathing in a sheltered and concealed portion of the sandy beach on the island's east end.

"Sweet," said Henry. "I think we should make our way to the beach tomorrow and meet these girls. They are probably staying for the summer at one of the mansions on the southeast shore, or they are working at one of the hotels."

"I'm up for it. There nothing else to do on this shitty rock," Rufus said.

"Hey, dude. Have the police talked to you about that girl who died?" Bryant said.

"Yeah," said Rufus, enjoying a joint. "A lady detective. I sent her a copy of the video. All I heard was a scream. Didn't see anything."

"It's still creepy that you were so close to where a murder took place. The article on the internet says she was strangled and raped."

"Any idea of who she was?" Henry said.

"My dad thinks she may have been a runaway from New York or Boston," Rufus said. "But how did she get here and where was she staying? Nobody knows. Shit happens."

***

"I'm already bored and I've just been here two days," Lucy Reynolds said. Sitting next to her on the porch of the grand Moose Island home where her parents spent every summer was her friend Ava Everett. Both girls were juniors in high school in Brookline, Massachusetts. Ava's parents' home sat next to that of Lucy, separated only by an impeccably manicured lawn that sloped down to the rocky shore. Their respective families lived in the island's exclusive Lighthouse Estates.

"I'll be glad when I go to college. I can spend summers where I want," Ava said.

"You don't think your parents will try to drag you here even then?"

"They can try, but I can refuse. I'll be a legal adult."

"Good luck with that," Lucy said.

"Let's head down to the beach. I know a place where we can go topless."

"How do you know that?"

"I ran into one of the waitresses who works at the Sea Breeze hotel. She goes to college at Brown and works here in the summer. She told me about it."

"There's also a place where we can go sea kayaking. We need some outdoor activities or we'll go mad here," Lucy said. "As for boys, this island doesn't have much to offer."

"But there is alcohol and other pharmaceutical products," Ava said. "We can't be working on our tans all of the time."

***

Dave Carr scanned his text messages. Chuck should have been here by now, Dave thought. He was hoping to hear from his friend Chuck Billings, who had told him he was planning to return soon to Moose Island from his home port in Marblehead, Massachusetts. Billings had last sailed up to Moose Island three days ago, but then turned around and returned to Marblehead. Dave and Natalie had texted Billings that they had been pleased with the present he had left behind. Billings and his wife Claire were close friends with Dave and Natalie.

"How many reservations do we have for the morning?" Dave said.

"Four. A couple from New Hampshire and two girls," Natalie replied. "Looks like the girls are here now."

Dave looked up from his fleet of kayaks to see the two girls approaching. His eyes immediately veered toward their tan, shapely legs. It would be a good morning, he said to himself.

7

After Ava and Lucy returned from their sea kayak excursion, they had planned to return home and spend the rest of the day sunbathing on the beach. But as they started walking back from the dock, Dave and Natalie asked them if they would like to attend a party on Friday at the Billings's home.

"Chuck and Claire know both of your parents. They'll be invited, too. But the party won't be just for adults. Chuck employs a couple of girls your age on the crew of his sailboat. They'll be there. And if you wanted to invite any of the islanders, you're welcome to," Dave said.

"Thanks," Ava said. "It's about time that someone livened up this island."

As Ava and Lucy walked on the path back to their houses, they ran into Rufus, Bryant, and Henry. The group chatted for a few minutes. Ava eventually informed the boys about the party. They all enthusiastically agreed to attend.

After the girls had departed, Rufus expressed some concern.

"I'm not sure my parents will let me go. They don't know or socialize with the families who live in the Lighthouse Estates," Rufus said.

"Simple. Don't tell them you're going. Just say you're hanging out with us. Lying to your parents is simple. I do it all the time," Henry said.

"Do you tell them that you drink beer and smoke pot?" Bryant said.

"No," Rufus said. "I'm not an idiot."

"Then you already lie to them. What's the harm in another lie?" Bryant said.

"I guess I'm overly cautious."

"Get over it, dude."

"Those girls were hot. And I bet there will be more at the party just like them," Bryant said. "I plan to get me some."

***

Chuck Billings was the CEO of Billings Venture Capital. In addition to owning a second home on Moose Island, he also was the captain of a fifty-foot sailboat that he used to cruise up and down the east coast. His family had owned property on the island for three generations. He and the other people who lived in the exclusive Lighthouse Estates enclave employed many full-time islanders to maintain their lawns and clean their houses. But they only socialized with their own tribe.

On the night of the party, the adults stayed primarily in the great room of the house that Chuck and his wife Claire owned. The well-heeled guests talked about their investments, world travels, and high-profile divorces in Boston or New York City.

A group of teenagers congregated in and around the heated pool. Ava and Lucy chatted with the two girls who worked on Billings's sailboat. The female crew members were coy about how they got their positions on the boat and what they did exactly. But they did seem to have an ample supply of drugs to dispense if anyone asked.

"That girl Chloe wants me to join her in the boat," Ava said. "Want to join us?"

"I'd rather hang out with Bryant," Lucy said.

"A budding romance?"

"Shut up. Just go and do whatever you plan to do."

"Suit yourself," Ava said.

***

Rufus was uncomfortable the entire time he was at the party. He was not by nature social, especially around teenage girls. He preferred to spend his time alone with his phone and computer. He was most comfortable only with Henry and Bryant; they had become his best friends since he moved to the island. He feared what would happen when they left the island to attend college. Although he talked a big game about girls, the truth was that he was shy and nervous around them, especially the ones who displayed their budding sexuality most provocatively.

Standing off to the side and trying to remain inconspicuous, Rufus slyly turned on the camera on his phone to record the evening's events, some of which would make it onto his YouTube channel, whereas other scenes would remain for his private viewing. He recorded the girl named Ava wandering down the dock with another girl and boarding the huge sailboat. They disappeared below deck. Then Rufus saw his friend Bryant leaving with the girl named Lucy. Except for him, no one noticed that they had left. Rufus followed inconspicuously behind the pair as they walked away from the house and onto a little-known path that traversed the length of the island. Only locals knew it was there. It was not on any tourist map.

Rufus wondered where the two were heading. Then he realized that Bryant was escorting Lucy to the run-down artist's cottage where the boys met. This turn of events didn't seem right to Rufus, who always felt that the cottage was a special place just for him and his male friends. He saw them entering the cottage. He crept slowly up to a window, making sure that he was using the night-time setting for his camera. He taped the pair having sex. He turned off his camera and returned home. On his walk back home through the woods, he thought he heard branches breaking and the voices of several people. But he didn't encounter anyone else on the unmarked trail. Back in his room, he watched over and over again the video that he had recorded that evening.

***

Nadine dreamed that she was floating above the island like an albatross when she was suddenly awaked by a repetitive knock on her door. She opened her eyes. Sunshine streamed through the window and slashed across the quilt on her bed.

"Who is it?" she said groggily.

"It's me: Mitzi. Please come downstairs. Julien is here. It's important."

Nadine threw on a hoodie and followed Mitzi downstairs in her bare feet.

"Nadine," Julien said, standing before her shirtless and sweating. "I found the body of a young woman washed up on Puffin Beach this morning while I was having my morning run. She's dead. I moved her farther up on shore above the tide line, and covered her with my shirt. You better make a call to the mainland."

"Shit," Nadine muttered. "Let me get some shoes. Take me there."

8

"The young woman you found on the beach is named Ava Everett, age seventeen," Nadine said to Julien later that day. "Her parents didn't even know she was missing until I started canvassing the Lighthouse Estates. Her mother said the last time she saw her she was partying with friends at the house of Chuck Billings. She admitted that she and her husband stumbled home drunk at about two o'clock in the morning. They never even bothered checking on the whereabouts of their daughter."

"Unbelievable," Julien said, shaking his head disgustedly. "When I found her, I didn't see any visible wounds on her body."

"It looks like a drowning," Nadine said. "The body was taken to the state medical examiner's office."

"Have you begun interviewing the people who were at this party?"

"I'm starting this morning with the teenagers. I've assembled a list of people who were at this party."

"Good luck," Julien said.

The first person to whom Nadine wanted to speak was Rufus Nugent. He seemed to always be around when something happened, Nadine thought. She found Rufus sitting on the back porch of his house.

"Hello, Rufus. We meet again. You were at the party, correct?"

"Yes. I'm already in enough trouble because my parents found out I was there when I told them I wasn't going."

"That's the least of your trouble if you don't tell me everything you heard or saw. Did you videotape anything last night?"

Rufus hesitated before answering.

"Yes."

"Phone please."

Nadine began watching footage of teenagers jumping in and out of a heated pool and going in and out of the shadows. Then the camera followed a couple through the woods.

"Who are these people, Rufus?"

"It has nothing to do with what happened to that girl. It was stupid what I did. Stop watching it please."

"What did you record?"

"My friend Bryant having sex with this girl Lucy whom he met at the party. It was a dumb thing to do, I know. Lucy was with Ava, however. That's important, right? Here, let me show you something."

Nadine handed the phone back to Rufus. He pulled up a portion of the video that showed Ava leaving the party and heading toward the sailboat.

"Do you know who that other girl is?"

"Yeah, her name is Chloe. She said she worked on the sailboat. Look, they both get on the boat, and then they go below deck. Here, look."

Nadine noticed that the camera panned away from the boat back to the house.

"Wait, replay that portion of the footage."

Nadine saw a figure getting on the sailboat after the girls had disappeared below deck.

"Did one of the boys at the party follow the girls onto the boat?'

"Not while I was there. I don't know who that other person was."

"You need to send me this file, Rufus."

"All of it?"

"All of it."

"You don't have to show anyone the portion with Bryant and Lucy, do you? And my parents don't have to know, right?"

"I don't think it's relevant. But my advice to you is to stop invading other people's privacy. That's a surefire way to lose friends. And erase that video from your phone after you send the file to me."

Rufus nodded knowingly and with a great deal of embarrassment. Nadine then headed to where Billings's sailboat was docked to speak with this girl Chloe. Before Nadine had a chance to talk to the girl, however, she received a call from Captain Davies.

"We have identified the first Moose Island victim: a sixteen-year-old runaway from suburban Boston. Her name is Harlow Williams. Her parents hadn't heard from her in over two weeks, but they saw the news coverage about the dead girl on Moose Island. Since you were busy with the investigation, their inquiry was routed to me. I met them in Augusta, where they positively identified their daughter," Davies said.

"Where do they live?"

"In Marblehead."

"So, they have money."

"It would appear that way. Their daughter was also hooked on opiates. They wanted to put her in rehab. But she ran away before they could take her to a private facility in New Hampshire."

"How did she get to Moose Island?" Nadine said. "She didn't drive there."

"I confirmed with her parents that she didn't steal any of the family cars. And there are no buses or trains that would have taken her anywhere near the island. She could have hitchhiked, I guess."

"Possible, but unlikely," Nadine said. "Thanks for the confirmation. I'm still waiting to learn the cause of death for Ava Everett."

"I'll make sure the medical examiner makes it a priority."

After finishing the call with Davies, Nadine continued on to the Billings's property, where she spotted two young women on the boat's deck. One was blond and the other a red head.

"I'm Detective Nadine McAfee. Which one of you is Chloe?"

"I am," said the blond.

"I have witnesses saying that you came on this boat with Ava last night. What happened? What do you know about how she died?"

"Nothing," Chloe said. "Yes, we came aboard to smoke some weed. But after about an hour I left and that was the last time I ever saw her. She was pretty wasted. But I was shocked when I heard she had drowned. I don't know where she went after I left the boat."

"What's your name?" Nadine said to the other woman.

"Amber."

"Did you see or talk to Ava last night?"

"I saw her at the pool. But we really didn't talk."

"What do the two of you do on this boat?"

"Mr. Billings hired us for the summer to cook and keep the boat clean. He goes back and forth between here and Marblehead during the summer," Chloe said.

"Sounds like a great way to spend the summer."

"It is," Amber said.

"Is Mr. Billings home?"

"Yes. He came and checked on us this morning after we all learned about Ava's drowning. He's a nice man. He was very concerned about us," Chloe volunteered.

Nadine ascended the manicured lawn to the imposing house that sat above the private dock. There, she met Chuck and Claire Billings. After offering Nadine a cup of coffee, Claire retreated to the kitchen, leaving Chuck and Nadine in the living room with its stunning view of the sea.

"It's tragic what happened to Ava," Billings said.

"Did you know her?"

"Yes, of course. Her parents' house is located just down the coast a few hundred yards. They must be devastated. Claire and I don't have children, but I can only imagine the pain they are experiencing."

"There was a group of teenagers at the party. Did you invite them?"

"No, not really. The party was initially meant to be for our adult friends. But word gets around on this small island. The kids just showed up. But I was fine with them hanging around the pool. There's not much else to do on this island for teenagers. I didn't recognize some of them. Must have been locals. Do you think that one of the locals could have been involved?"

"Why would you think that?"

"I don't know. But there has always been tension between the locals and those of us who just spend summers here."

"I'm investigating all possibilities."

"I'm sure you are."

"Do you often hire teenagers to travel with you on your sailboat in the summer?"

"Just in the past two summers. My wife suggested it. It's a great way for kids to learn how to sail and make some money doing it."

"Amber and Chloe said that they clean and cook."

"Yes, but I also give them sailing lessons."

"A forensics team will be arriving on the afternoon ferry. I need to have them comb through your boat, since that's where Ava was last seen alive," Nadine said.

"Of course. Do what you need to do."

Nadine then interviewed Ava's friend Lucy, who could barely make it through their conversation without crying every five minutes. Lucy told Nadine about her liaison with Bryant, and that she hadn't seen Ava after she left the party.

"How did you learn about the party?"

"Ava and I went sea kayaking yesterday. The owner Mr. Carr told us about it. He invited us," Lucy said.

Nadine thought it was odd that someone other than Billings had taken it upon himself to invite the girls to the party that he wasn't hosting. She added Carr to the list of people she needed to interview. She then looked at the time. Julien and his wife had invited her to their house for dinner. She scrambled to purchase a bottle of wine and headed to their house.

"What do you know about Chuck Billings?" Nadine said.

"Not much. Other than he has a large boat and an even larger house. I imagine his ego matches both."

"I learned that Ava and her friend Lucy were invited to the party by a man named Carr, who runs a sea kayak business."

"We know Dave and his wife Natalie a little. I wouldn't say we're friends. They're nice, but they keep to themselves mostly. Some people like their privacy."

"But he knew about the party."

"I don't know how he became friendly with Billings. It's none of my business."

"Do you know what Carr did before coming to the island?"

"He told us that taught Russian at Williams College. That's about all I was ever able to get out of him. Like I said: he likes his privacy. But let's not talk shop anymore. Have some more wine."

As Nadine was saying her goodbyes later than evening, her phone buzzed. She looked at Julien and Julia. Her expression turned grim.

"Ava Everett was strangled and raped. She did not drown," Nadine said.

"There's a serial killer on this island," Julien said. "Fucking hell."

9

The pressure ramped up on Nadine to solve the murders on Moose Island before another woman was assaulted. Young women who worked at the various bed-and-breakfast establishments and the Sea Breeze hotel now walked to and from work in pairs. Residents began locking their doors and windows. Tourist traffic on the ferry diminished as news of the murders spread.

Two days after Ava's body was discovered, Nadine did receive some good news that would help move the investigation forward. The semen found in the bodies of both Harlow and Ava matched. Nadine now had evidence that one man was responsible for the two rapes and murders. Nadine's first thought was that Chuck Billings could have assaulted the women. But that theory fell apart when Nadine was able to verify that Billings was not on the island when Harlow was killed. In digging into the movements of Billings, however, Nadine was able to verify that he left Marblehead three days before Harlow was discovered sprawled at the bottom of the cliff, but then he returned from Moose Island the following day. Moreover, the harbormaster in Marblehead told Nadine that he recalled seeing three young women board the boat with Billings and his wife on that quick trip up the coast, but that only two women were on the boat when it had returned and then set sail again for Moose Island.

Nadine also dug into the backgrounds of Dave and Natalie Carr. To her surprise, she discovered that neither one had taught at Williams College. They both had been lying about their past.

Nadine visited Chloe and Amber once again. She discovered them bringing provisions onto the sailboat.

"What are you doing?" Nadine said.

"Mr. Billings told us to prepare to sail. We're leaving tomorrow," Chloe explained.

"Did you pick up a girl in Marblehead about five days ago?"

"I don't know what you're talking about."

"I have a witness who told me that another girl joined you on the sail up from Massachusetts. Was her name Harlow?"

Amber and Chloe looked at each other, remaining silent.

"The girl was murdered. If you know anything about her, you have to tell me. I don't know what Billings has threatened you with, but you need to tell me the truth," Nadine said forcefully.

"We can't say anything," Amber said.

"Where is Billings now?"

"He left to pick up some supplies at the general store."

"You two are staying with me," Nadine said.

Nadine then made a call to Julien, explaining to him her suspicions about Billings, and asking for his help.

"I suspect that Billings may be involved in sex trafficking. I'm bringing over to you two girls from his boat. They're afraid to talk, so would you look after them while I track down Billings?"

"Of course," Julien said.

Nadine escorted Chloe and Amber to Julien's store. Then she headed to the dock, where she spoke with Phil Nugent.

"Yeah, Billings was just here buying supplies, along with Dave Carr and his wife. They told me they were heading off on a week-long sail up the coast to Nova Scotia," Phil said.

Nadine then called Julien again.

"Can you leave your wife in charge of the store and the two girls and help me find Billings and Carr?" Nadine said. "They're preparing to flee the island and head for Canada. I know you're not a cop anymore. But I can't get backup here to the island fast enough."

"Yes, of course," Julien said. "It's not like I forgot how to be a cop. But I'm confused about something. You mentioned Dave Carr. How is he involved in all of this?"

"I found that he and his wife never taught at Williams College," Nadine said. "I don't know what their real story is. But I'm assuming that both of them are a threat."

"I'll meet you where two trails intersect at the community church. Should I bring my gun?" Julien said.

"That might be wise," Nadine said.

Nadine and Julien met at the crossroads near the church and headed toward Lighthouse Estates.

"Did the girls say anything to you?" Nadine said.

"I told them I used to be a detective," Julien said. "But they remained silent. They seem really scared. Maybe they'll speak to my wife."

"Look up ahead. I see Billings and Carr loading supplies onto the boat."

Nadine and Julien rushed toward the sailboat with guns drawn.

"No need for a firefight," Billings said calmly. Billings, Carr, and their respective spouses stood silently before Nadine and Julien.

"I'm arresting both of you on suspicion of the rape and murder of Harlow Williams and Ava Everett," Nadine said.

"You'll regret saying those words," Carr said calmly.

"Why is that?"

"You'll find out soon enough."

Nadine looked at Julien. Both thought that Carr was showing misplaced bravado. Nadine called the mainland for additional officers and a boat to take Carr and Billings to the nearest county jail in Colby.

Nadine obtained saliva samples from both men that would show who raped the two women. While she waited for the results, Captain Davies called her into his office. When she walked in, she saw two men in suits already there.

"Nadine, these are special agents Taylor and Cochran from the FBI's counter intelligence unit," Davies said.

"What's this all about?" Nadine said.

"Detective McAfee, we're here to retrieve Mr. Carr. He's under our control as part of the witness protection program," Agent Taylor said. "He needs to be relocated."

"What? You're fucking kidding me, right? But you just can't take him. He could be involved in two rapes and murders," Nadine said. "What's his real name? I found out myself that he never taught at Williams College."

"His name is Dimitry Kholkhalov. He's a double agent who has been giving the U.S. government valuable information about Russian spy operations in this country. He is scheduled to testify before several federal grand juries in New York and Washington in the next few months. But if you move forward with prosecuting him here on rape and murder charges, he will refuse to testify," Taylor explained. "We can't have that. We can't have years of work jeopardized."

"What about the young women who were his victims? Has he ever done anything like this before?"

"We knew that he and his wife liked playing sex games with younger women. They had a history of this back in Moscow as well."

"How was Billings involved in this?"

"Billings procured the women for Carr," Taylor said.

"And he'll get off as well?"

"He has powerful friends in Washington. He'll make sure that the two women on his boat will be compensated generously for maintaining their silence."

"Captain, you can't be OK with all of this?"

"I'm not," Davies said. "But I was informed unequivocally that, officially, the arrests of Carr and Billings never happened. They're going to be released into the custody of the FBI."

"And what am I going to tell the parents of Harlow and Ava? The two dead girls. Remember them?"

"You're going to tell them that you found the killer," Agent Cochran chimed in.

"What are you talking about?"

"In two days, the body of a man will wash up on the shore of Moose Island, along with an abandoned small sailboat," Cochran explained. "The man's blood will have a high concentration of opiates. His DNA will match that found in the bodily fluids found in your victims. There's your killer. He had been prowling around Moose Island, coming on shore looking for young women to assault and then heading out to sea to escape detection. Before he could attack again, he overdosed, fell off of his boat, and then drowned."

"But his DNA will not match that of the real killer, which will either be Billings or Carr. But based on what you told me, probably Carr's, or whatever his name is," Nadine said.

"The mouth swabs you took yesterday were lost, unfortunately," Taylor said. "Plus, you have no witnesses."

"I can't be a part of this," Nadine said.

"This is bigger than both of us, Nadine," Davies said.

"You just conveniently found a dead man to play the role of the killer?"

"The man who will be found in two days was an expendable resource," Taylor said. "Look, we can't bring the two women back to life. But you can tell the parents and the Moose Island community that the killer is now dead. Closure will be had. Calm will be restored."

"And it'll all be a lie," Nadine said. "And what makes you so certain that Carr won't do this again in whatever community you put him in next as part of witness protection?"

"We'll be watching him more carefully after he testifies."

"Good to know," Nadine said. "And what makes you think they I'll remain quiet about all of this cloak-and-dagger shit?"

"Just imagine what we could do to your life and career," Taylor said. "Just imagine."

"Captain, I believe we are done here," Cochran said.

After the agents departed, Nadine looked at Davies with fury in her eyes.

"Let it go, Nadine. Just let it go."

10

Two weeks after the FBI whisked Dave Carr and his wife away to an undisclosed location, Nadine was still fuming with their decision to protect him and absolve him from crimes he likely committed. Captain Davies suggested that it would be a good time for her to take a vacation so she could work through her anger. Nadine decided to take her grandmother Martha to Moose Island to spend a week in a cottage that she had rented. Martha was delighted at the prospective of getting out of her house and spending time by the ocean.

While on the island, Nadine introduced Martha to Julien and Julia. Martha and Julia especially hit it off. Martha introduced Julia to her special recipes for oatmeal cookies and blueberry pie, both of which Julia planned to add to her menu at the sandwich shop.

One day, while Julia and Martha spent time in the kitchen, Nadine and Julien sat on the back porch having a few beers. The early July weather was hot, even with a sea breeze.

"What are the locals saying about the sudden departure of the Carrs?" Nadine asked.

"The Carrs returned for a few days to tell everyone that they decided to shutter their business and travel the world for the next year. Their inventory of kayaks was left to a guy named Devin, who may or may not reopen the business," Julien said. "Most people just shrugged at the news. They were still buzzing about the fact that the real killer had been found."

"Real killer my ass," Nadine said.

"Those counter-intelligence guys know how to clean up a mess. I had a few run-ins with them during my time in Boston. They don't fuck around."

"You can't feel good about Carr and Billings getting away with their crimes."

"I don't feel good at all. It's been nagging at me. Although we'll never know for sure now, I suspect that it was Carr who killed the women. Billings just procured them for him," Julien said.

"That's my conclusion also," Nadine agreed.

"You know, Billings is still here on the island."

"You've got to be kidding me."

"Oh, yeah. A man with his connections has no shame. He's rich enough to buy himself anything and rich enough to get himself out of any jam," Julien said. Then he paused and took a sip from her beer bottle. "But there is a way to serve up some justice to a man like Billings."

"How's that?"

"Now, before I tell you about what I've been thinking, you are free to refuse participation in my plan or pretend you never heard it."

"Understood. Continue."

Nadine listened as Julien unraveled his idea for getting back at Chuck Billings. Later that night, Julien told Julia and Martha that he and Nadine were going to walk to the cliffs near the southeast corner of the island to get some fresh air. Julien grabbed two containers of gasoline from the storage shed behind his house.

"Even though it's dark, we can't be walking across the island carrying two large red gas cans," Nadine warned.

"There's a path that only locals know about."

"It's pitch dark out here. Are we taking the headlamps?"

"Don't need them. Just follow close behind me and try to avoid the tree roots."

Nadine and Julien walked through a narrow, weed-clogged trail until they emerged behind the Lighthouse Estates. They maneuvered quietly behind the grand homes until they saw where Billings and his wife lived. Down a slope they saw his sailboat gently bobbing in the water.

"I don't want any deaths on my hands or conscience," Nadine said.

"No one is going to get hurt. You go down and set the boat on fire first. Once Billings and his wife see the blaze, they will come running out of their house. That's when I torch their home," Julien said. "Now go."

As Nadine crept toward the sailboat, she had to sweep away from her mind a sense of guilt at what she was about to do. Not to mention the ethical quandary of a detective becoming an arsonist. The boat was dark and Nadine saw no movement on it. She emptied her can of gasoline on the deck, then she lit a rag and tossed it on board, sparking the fire. She then ran back toward the trail.

As she crouched in the bushes, she first heard screams and then frantic yelling. Billings and his wife Claire sprinted toward their boat. Shortly after that, she saw a burst of flame coming from the house.

Moose Island had one small fire truck that could throw a few hundred gallons of water on a blaze, but it was essentially useless against a large fire. As Nadine and Julien crept back to his house on the trail, they heard the truck's siren.

"What's going on out there?" Julia said.

"Looks like there's a fire down at the Lighthouse Estates," Julien said. "We saw some of the volunteer fire crew scrambling to get over there. Fortunately, the breeze will take the embers out to sea and away from other homes."

"So, we're OK here?" Martha said.

"Yes. There's no need to evacuate down to the dock, which is what the islanders have been instructed to do if a fire on the island ever got out of hand."

"Do you know whose house is burning?" Julia said.

"No. Have no idea. I suppose we'll find out soon enough. News travels fast on Moose Island," Julien said.

"What do you say, Nadine? Would you like another beer?"

"I'd love one. It's a beautiful night. Just look at those stars, Grandma. Aren't they amazing?"

"It's glorious here," Martha said.

"We hope you two make it a point to return," Julia said.

"I'd love to spend more time here," Nadine said. "There's something special about this place."

"That's what we've found. Cheers, everyone," Julien said.

Later that night as Nadine lay in bed, a faint smell of charred wood wafted through an open window of her rented cottage. She smiled, turned over onto her side, and slept peacefully.

PART 2: SIZING UP THE NEWCOMERS

11

The residents of Moose Island, both the newly minted and the old timers, were surprised that the ramshackle artist's cottage in one of the most remote locations on the island was sold and was being made livable once again. For Rufus Nugent and his teenage friends, this meant that they had lost their secret location to drink, smoke weed, and engage in the rare sexual encounter.

About one month after the fire destroyed the Billings's boat and home, sending them packing back to Massachusetts, the New York-based artist Wendy Wiseman arrived on the island, having purchased the cottage from the remaining living relative of the old man who had once owned the cottage and the small plot of land on which it sat.

Few people on the island had ever heard of Wendy Wiseman. The exceptions being a small cadre of local artists who knew about her reputation as being a purple-haired eccentric who nevertheless had set the modern art world on fire with her eye-popping colorful abstract works that were garnished by ancient mystical symbols. Moreover, she was married to the best-selling author Norman Manson, whose novels of middle-class angst in the twentieth century were compared to those of John Cheever. The curious thing about their relationship was that, even though they were married, they lived apart. Wagging tongues on the island learned that, although Wendy had purchased the cottage for herself, Norman had rented a cottage on the opposite end of the island, just two lots over from where Julien and Julia Pelletier lived.

"How do you know all of this?" Julien asked his wife.

"I ran into Mitzi at the store," Julia said. "She told me that her friend Irma, the real-estate agent, handled both the house sale and the rental contract."

"Of course, it had to be Mitzi," Julien sighed.

"Someone has to be the island busy body," Julia laughed. "Has Nadine any leads on the arsonist?"

"Nope," Julien said. "The state fire marshal confirmed that the blazes were both intentionally set. But no evidence has been found that could lead to a suspect."

"Could it have been one of the teenagers on the island?"

"Who knows? It could also have been one of the summer kids playing a prank that got out of hand."

"It's going to be a hot one today. The island should be packed. I've already planned for extra lunch goers."

"And I'm all set with our inventory," Julien said.

He and Nadine had vowed never to mention the fires that they had set. It was a criminal act to be sure, but one they felt was warranted given the circumstances. Neither felt any remorse towards or sympathy for Chuck Billings.

***

Less than a month after Wendy had purchased the cottage, it was habitable. She had hired a crew from the mainland to work on the island and complete the work as fast as possible. Rufus was the first person to notice that Wendy had moved in. On one of his daily rambles across the island, he spotted her painting a symbol on the wooden siding near the front door. Wendy heard movement in the woods and called out. Rufus appeared from the forest to greet her.

"Hi, my name's Rufus."

"Nice to meet you, Rufus. I'm Wendy."

On seeing her for the first time, Rufus was struck not only by the purple hair but how attractive she was, even though, at least to his teenage mind, she was probably in her forties. She wore shorts that showed off her long, tanned legs and a T-shirt that did little to hide her fulsome breasts.

"I know this place," Rufus said.

"How's that?"

"My friends and I used to hang out here."

"Doing what?"

"You know: guy stuff."

"You mean beer and weed."

"Exactly."

"Sorry to take away your special place. I'm sure you can find other places for your teenage debauchery," Wendy said.

"What's that you're painting?"

"It's called a pentagram. It's a Druid symbol. The five points of the pentagram radiate positive energy outward as both a blessing and protection for my house and land," Wendy explained.

"Are you a Druid?'

"I guess you could say I'm a modern Druid. I believe in reverence for the natural world. I want to be in. harmony with it. That's why I had to finally move from my loft in Brooklyn to here. I needed to renew my spirit."

"Cool," Rufus said.

"If you don't mind, I'd like to finish my work. But you're welcome to come back. I can tell you more about Druidism if you're really interested."

"Thanks. I might do that."

After Rufus retreated back into the woods, he immediately texted his friends Henry and Bryant about the crazy artist with the hot body.

***

On the other side of the island Norman Manson settled into his rental house. He had brought ten boxes of books with him. He gave an extra twenty dollars to the man who brought the books to the cottage in his ATV. With an exception made for a small fire truck, there were no cars or other large vehicles allowed on the island. The cottage smelled like dirty socks, Manson thought. He opened a window, but just more humid air rushed in. There was no air conditioning, but there was a ceiling fan. Thank God, he muttered to himself as he searched for a pair of shorts to slip on. He wasn't sure how he would be able to finish his latest book by Thanksgiving in these conditions, he thought.

He stopped unpacking to sit down. Drenched in sweat, he found his cell phone.

"Well, I'm here. I feel like I'm in one of those nineteenth-century French prisons off the coast of South America," he said.

"It can't be that bad," a woman's voice on the other end said.

"All I can see is trees. Wendy's the tree lover, not me."

"Then leave her. You know that's what I want."

"It's not the right time," Norman said. "When can you come to the island?"

"I can get away in about a week. I want to close on this townhouse in the Upper West Side."

"I need you, Charlotte."

"You'll have me. Just be patient."

Shortly after ending his call with Charlotte, Wendy burst through the door, startling him.

"Have you ever heard of the tradition of knocking? I hear it goes back centuries," Norman said.

"Settling in? This place is quaint. Quirky."

"Not the words I would use."

"You'll adjust. Would you like me to stay the night?" Wendy said, slipping her arms around her neck.

"Not tonight. It's too damn hot."

"You can fuck me on grass behind the house. No one will see us."

"A delicious prospect, but not the most propitious timing," Norman said. "Another time."

"Suit yourself. Come over to my cottage tomorrow."

"I look forward to it," Norman said.

On her way back to her cottage, Wendy did not notice that Rufus was filming her from a hidden location on the trees.

12

In his youth, Norman Manson cut a handsome figure in the New York City literary universe. Tall with obsessively combed brown hair and piercing green eyes, he burst upon the scene like a comet after graduating from Columbia University. His first three novels which focused on doomed love affairs and misplaced morals among the upper-class were best sellers in the late 1990s and early 2000s. But his last two novels were largely ignored by critics and readers. His large advances and sales had withered along with his first two marriages.

His brown hair had grayed and thinned and his lean physique had grown rounder. His moods had become darker. He saw his sun setting. That's when he met

Wendy at a party in Brooklyn to which his editor had invited him. While not as famous as he once was, he still possessed a charm and masculine magnetism that drew women to him. And many people still remembered his first books just as audiences knew the words to the earliest songs of fading rock stars. Norman cringed when people came up to him and asked: "What have you been doing these past fifteen years?" He would like to have responded: "Writing books, you motherfucker. If you had bought them, we wouldn't be having this conversation." His remaining morsel of social graces stopped him from such an outburst, however.

After meeting Wendy, he knew that if he hitched himself to her rising star, he might regain relevance. But he also realized that he had to write a work that was worthy of the reading public's attention. The very first time he spent alone with Wendy he learned of her devotion to Druidism, that ancient Celtic religion that Norman thought only attracted crackpots. But Wendy was no crackpot. She took her art seriously, and she had become seriously rich because of it. Norman could tolerate her eccentricities when she had the money to subsidize their lifestyle. Within six months of their first meeting, they were wed, first in a civil ceremony in New York, and then in a Druid ceremony in a forest in the Adirondacks in upstate New York. Norman felt like a fool wearing a white robe and a crown made from oak branches, but he tolerated the indignity to appease Wendy. He also had to admit that her sexual energy was invigorating for a man about to cross to the far side of fifty. Their encounters were delicious when they were actually together. Wendy insisted that they live separately because she needed to cultivate her own energy to do her best work. "As a creative artist yourself, I hope you understand the need for a room of my own," she said.

Part of Norman did understand her perspective, but the time he did spend with her ignited his sexual desires. Desires that Wendy couldn't fulfill when they were apart. Then he met an attractive real estate agent named Charlotte Yeager while he was browsing in a bookstore near Central Park. They struck up an affair shortly after meeting. Charlotte, a willowy blond with a degree in history from Smith, dressed impeccably. But probably equally if not more important for Norman, she loved his work. She wanted to be with him. Now Norman was torn between his admiration for a recognized artistic genius with a quirky personality who wanted to live on an island in the middle of nowhere, and a stable, practical woman with whom he could live in Manhattan. For the moment, however, Wendy held the purse strings. And he had a novel to write in his rustic cottage. Divorce could come later. He focused now on crafting words and a story that somebody other than himself would care about.

The first week on Moose Island did not go well for Norman. He couldn't write. It was too quiet for him. He was used to the pulsating rhythm of New York, not the sublime quiet of an island off of the coast of Maine. He went out several times a day to buy food. He didn't cook. He became a frequent customer of the High Tide sandwich shop, where he enjoyed the daily offerings of Julia Pelletier.

Four days into his stay, he noticed that a note had been slipped under the door of his cottage. Wendy had invited him over to her retreat. She had also left him a map so he could navigate there. When he finally arrived, he was sweating and his right knee was bleeding after having tripped over some tree roots.

"Let me clean that up for you," Wendy said.

"This fucking place can kill you," Norman said, wincing from the organic balm that Wendy placed on his injured knee.

"How's your book coming?" Wendy asked.

"About like my knee. Only pain," he said. "Do we really have to stay here?"

"Yes, I do. You can leave if you want."

"You know that I can't afford to be anywhere else right now."

"Then I guess you're staying."

"For how long?"

"Maybe forever," she said. "But there are compensations."

"Such as?"

Wendy then disrobed and stood naked in front of Norman. As he lay next to her, all he could think about was the blank pages waiting for him when he returned to his cottage. No amount of Wendy's sensual delights could help with that.

13

After just one week on Moose Island, Norman had become a fixture for lunch at the High Tide sandwich shop. Julia told Julien about the writer who sat at the table with a yellow legal tablet at one o'clock each day.

"He always orders a grilled chicken sandwich," Julia said.

"Some people like routine in their lives," Julien said.

"He's the husband of that female artist who bought the run-down cottage."

"Really?"

"But they don't live together. What's up with that?"

"Don't you become an island gossip now," Julien warned.

"I just listen and observe," Julia said. "I told him you were an ex-detective. He'd like to meet you."

"No, thanks."

"Just step out of the shop for a moment tomorrow and say hello. Be island friendly."

The following day, to appease Julia, Julien popped in at the sandwich shop and introduced himself to Norman.

"My wife wanted me to say hello. I'm Julien Pelletier."

"Nice to meet you. I've never met a detective before."

"Consider yourself lucky."

"I'm struggling with my new book. I was hoping to include a murder in it. That would be a departure for me."

"I feel a bit embarrassed to say it, but I've never read your books," Julien said.

"Think nothing of it. My books are, shall I say, novels of upper-class manners. Not everyone's cup of tea."

"When I do read, I read history and biographies."

"A wise choice," Norman said. "If I can finally latch on to a storyline, would you mind if I picked your brain?"

"I don't mean to be rude, but I left the world of police work behind. I'm just a humble shopkeeper now."

"That's interesting in itself. Maybe I could use that in my book."

"Do whatever you want," Julien chuckled. "But I doubt that idea would turn into a bestseller. I have to get back to the shop. It was nice meeting you. Good luck."

Norman returned to his cottage. He was startled to find that a wasp that managed to infiltrate a screen. The barbed insect buzzed around his study. When it finally landed on a door, Norman grabbed a book and smashed it. That might be the only thing worthwhile I do today, he muttered to himself as he cleaned the carcass off the door.

But he was buoyed by the thought that Charlotte would be arriving tomorrow. So as not to arouse Wendy's suspicion, he arranged for Charlotte to spend three nights at the Sea Breeze hotel. He hoped that she would be the spark that would ignite his dormant creative fire.

***

Rufus did not tell his parents that he was spending time visiting Wendy at her artist's cottage. He also did not reveal that he was spending his summer vacation learning about Druidism.

"I read that Druids used to perform human sacrifices," Rufus said. "Julius Caesar wrote about it over two thousand years ago,"

"Yes, that's true," Wendy said.

"Caesar wrote about the wicker man, a human figure made of wood and straw. The Druids placed live human beings inside and then they set the wicker man on fire."

"This was all second-hand knowledge from the Romans," Wendy said.

"But it could be true."

"Possibly. We sometimes burn wooden effigies to celebrate the summer solstice. But that is rare, because it would draw attention to ourselves. We prefer to keep our celebrations private and peaceful. And, of course, there are modern fire codes that the ancient Celts did not have to worry about."

"I still think the wicker man is cool."

"You would," Wendy laughed.

Wendy returned to painting her flamboyantly colored canvas.

"What's the symbol you are drawing?"

"It's called the *vesica piscis*. It literally means the bladder of a fish. Since I'm living on an island now, I thought it appropriate to include it in my new commission.

The intertwining lines represent the union between man and woman, light and dark, heaven and Earth."

"Somebody already paid you for this?"

"Yes. And a lot of money. It's almost embarrassing. But a girl has got to live. Now if you wouldn't mind, I'd like to spend the rest of the afternoon alone."

"Sure. No problem," Rufus said.

***

"Dude, that artist is hot," said Rufus's friend Henry. Rufus had showed Henry and Bryant his secret videos that he took of Wendy at her cottage.

"Has she ever walked around nude?" Bryant asked.

"Not yet. But she's a fucking Druid. I bet she'll do it some time."

"Do you think she will have orgies there?" Henry asked.

"I'm ready to hit the record button if she does," Rufus said.

***

"Wendy, this is Sapphire. I have some news for you."

"About Norman?"

"Yes."

"Fill me in."

"Sources tell me that Charlotte Yeager is on her way to Moose Island."

"And Norman actually thought he could smuggle that bitch here," Wendy said.

"Do you want Daisy and I to come there?"

"Yes. Bring your tents and sleeping bags. You can camp next to my cottage. I have no room for guests inside. It's really cramped, even for me."

"We'll be there tomorrow."

"It will be nice to gather the priestesses together on this magical island."

14

After her flight from New York to Portland, Maine, Charlotte drove another three hours just to make it to the ferry in Stillwater Cove for the sea crossing to Moose Island. Exhausted by the time she walked up the hill to Sea Breeze hotel and checked in to her room that still had bathroom fixtures from the 1920s, she plopped down on the bed to compose herself. She and Norman had agreed to meet at seven o'clock in the hotel's restaurant, after which they would spend the night together in her hotel room.

When dinner time rolled around, she saw Norman walking in. She greeted him warmly with a kiss. For a place so isolated as Moose Island, Charlotte was impressed with the quality of the food. She admitted she was a New York snob when it came to dining. Separated from her husband, who was the vice president of a bank, she was drawn to the bleak seriousness of Norman. Even though his literary light had dimmed, she still saw him as the luminescent writer that he once was. He still retained most of the rugged handsomeness of the publicity photos that graced his once best-selling books. Charlotte preferred to be the lover of a serious writer rather than the spouse of a superficial banker.

As for Norman, he saw in Charlotte a responsible woman with a lucrative career in real estate. She clearly adored him and believed that he still had great work in him. It's not that Norman needed Charlotte to worship him, he just wanted her to stroke his ego, which was something that Wendy never did. Wendy lived in her own world; Norman lived on the fringes of it. Charlotte wanted to live with him and for him.

After finishing their meal, Norman suggested that they take a stroll to a small park near the ferry dock. The sun had begun to set and the air had cooled.

Neither Charlotte nor Norman noticed the figure who had been shadowing them since they left the hotel. As the couple retreated back into the warmth of the vintage hotel, the figure followed them, keeping a safe distance in the darkness. After Norman entered Charlotte's room, the figure entered the room right next to theirs, hoping to hear as much as possible through the thin walls.

***

Before Sapphire and Daisy arrived on Moose Island with their camping gear, Wendy purchased many bottles of wine. She also constructed a miniature wicker man to surprise her fellow Druids.

Wendy met her friends at the dock, escorting them through the winding path to her cottage as darkness began creeping down from the tops of the pine trees.

"We would never have found this place on our own," Daisy said.

"Let's get our tents up before it's completely dark," Sapphire suggested.

After assembling their lodgings behind Wendy's cottage, the women started a fire in the makeshift firepit that Wendy had assembled from rocks on her property. The wine and laughter flowed in equal measure until nearly midnight, when the tone of the evening changed.

"Is Charlotte on the island now?" Wendy said.

"Yes. We were on the same ferry with her. We know what she looks like, but she doesn't know who we are. We just looked like a couple of backpackers to her," Sapphire said.

"She and Norman are staying at the Sea Breeze hotel," Daisy said.

"I assume that they'll eventually migrate to his cottage," Wendy said.

"What's he been like since you've been on the island?' Sapphire said.

"Moody. Lacking confidence. He's not the man I once knew. He's become weak and needy."

"What are we going to do about it, my fellow priestesses?" Daisy said.

"I'm glad you asked. Wait one minute. Pour yourself some more wine," Wendy said. She then walked to her cottage, from which she emerged a minute later carrying a two-foot high wicker man that she assembled quickly from twigs she had picked up around her property. Upon seeing the wicker man, Sapphire and Daisy screamed with delight.

"That's absolutely wonderful," Daisy said. "You do the honors, Wendy."

Even though there was a damp chill in the air, Wendy disrobed and then placed the stick figure into the fire. The other women then shed their garments and began dancing around the fire as the wicker man burned. As the flames illuminated their naked bodies, the women began chanting: *Burn, burn, you betrayer/The one you loved is now your slayer.*

When the miniature wicker man had finally turned to ash, the women toasted its fiery demise.

"Let the cheating motherfucker rot in the flames of hell," Wendy said. This invective elicited a hearty cheer from the trio of women.

Cold and drunk, the women finally went to bed around one o'clock in the morning. Through all of their revelry, no one noticed a figure hiding in the woods behind the cottage. Rufus had slipped out of his house. He had videotaped the entire ceremony. He couldn't believe what he now had on his phone.

***

On the second day of Charlotte's sojourn on the island, Norman finally convinced her to spend one night at his cottage before she had to return to New York City.

"What if Wendy comes by unexpectedly?" Charlotte said.

"She won't," Norman said assuredly. "She's busy working on several new paintings. I won't see her for at least a week. Besides, I need your positive energy in my dingy little cottage."

"It can't be that bad."

Norman helped her pack her things and check out of the hotel.

"This is very nice, Norman. You had me expecting something like a cockroach-infested trailer home. This is clean and quaint," Charlotte said as she walked into Norman's cottage.

"I'm glad you like it. Pardon the piles of books on the floor. There's no place else to put them," he said. "As for dinner, I have wine and some sandwiches I bought at this place called the High Tide. I know it's not gourmet, but the sandwiches are delicious."

"That will be fine," Charlotte said, although she was skeptical of the choice of cuisine.

***

The morning after the wine-fueled ceremony with her friends, a slightly hungover Wendy knocked on the door of Norman's cottage several times before she decided to walk around to the back. She screamed when she saw Norman and Charlotte lying naked on the grass with their throats cut. Their arms were outstretched. Their hands had been impaled with sharp objects that looked like wooden spikes.

Not knowing for sure what to do next, she ran next door, trying to wake whomever lived there. No one answered. Then she ran to the adjoining house, where Julien Pelletier opened the door.

"Help me!" Wendy yelled.

"What's going on?" Julien said.

"Please. Follow me. My husband has been killed."

Julien followed Wendy to the cottage, where he saw the gruesome scene.

"Go back to my house. My wife is there," Julien ordered.

Making sure he kept his distance from the bodies, Julien fished around in his pocket for his phone and called Detective Nadine McAfee.

15

Nadine was bringing a cup of warm tea to her grandmother Martha when she received the call about the murders on Moose Island. Martha was nursing a summer cold, which she would always say is the worse kind of malady. "When it's summer, you want to be outside, not cooped up in bed," she said.

"Grandma, I have to leave for Moose Island to lead the investigation on a new case," Nadine said. "Can you manage by yourself? Or should I ask that the case be assigned to another detective?"

"You go, dear. I'll manage fine. It's merely a cold. I've chopped wood when it was thirty below zero while nursing a cold. This is nothing but a few sniffles."

"Whatever you say. You're the boss."

Nadine headed to the port in Stillwater Cove where she met the forensics team that was joining her on the island. She had already booked herself a room at the Albatross Inn, where she was sure the owner Mitzi already had her suspicions on who the murderer was.

The ferry arrived in the early afternoon. Nadine and the team headed straight to the crime scene, where she spotted Julien Pelletier, who had improvised with rope and a hand-painted sign a "no go" perimeter around Norman's cottage.

"Hi, Julien," Nadine said. "You were first on the scene?"

"Yes, along with the male victim's wife Wendy Wiseman."

"Who's the female victim?"

"According to Wendy, her name is Charlotte Yeager, who was apparently having an affair with Wendy's husband: Norman Manson."

"A messy situation all around," Nadine said. "Wait a second. Is this Norman Manson the writer?"

"The same."

"Shit. I used to like his books. I wondered whatever happened to him."

"Now you know," Julien said. "I have to return to the shop. Let me know how I can help."

Nadine nodded to Julien and motioned for the forensics team to begin their work. Nadine and the team recognized immediately that the couple had been killed in the bedroom, where the bed sheets were stained with blood. The killer then dragged the bodies downstairs and out onto the backyard.

"What is nailed through their hands?" Nadine asked a member of the team.

"It's a piece of wood that had been sharpened and then driven through their hands post-mortem."

"It looks like a ritualistic sacrifice," Nadine observed. "The bodies were staged."

"Yes. Something weird like that."

Nadine made sure she took photos of the bodies, the bedroom where the murders occurred, and the bloody trail from the bedroom to the backyard. She hoped that the killer was careless enough to have left behind fingerprints. When the forensics team had completed their work, the bodies were bagged and taken back to the mainland.

Before contacting Charlotte Yeager's husband, Nadine sought out Wendy. She followed Julien's directions to Wendy's cottage, where she was surprised to see two tents pitched behind it. Three women sat in chairs around a fire.

"I'm Detective McAfee. Who is Wendy Wiseman?"

"I am."

"I'm sorry for your loss. Can we go inside?"

"Of course."

Once inside, Nadine asked: "Who are those other women?"

"My friends Sapphire and Daisy. They have been here the past two days," Wendy said.

"Why was your husband staying at the cottage while you were here?"

"That was what we preferred in our relationship. We are both artists. We need our space. The arrangement works for us," Wendy said.

"When was the last time you saw your husband?"

"Four days ago. He spent the night here. In case you're wondering, we still have sex. We had sex that night."

"Did you know about the woman with whom he was having an affair?"

"You mean Charlotte? Yes, I recently found out about that."

"From whom?"

"You met them: Daisy and Sapphire. They live in New York City. They found out and told me. Gossip flies fast, whether it's on an island called Moose or Manhattan."

"How did that make you feel?"

"Our marriage was unconventional. I was surprised at first. But since I found out, I've come to terms with it. If Norman was still alive, I would have let him have his dalliance."

"But he's not alive. He was brutally murdered."

"I saw the bodies, Detective McAfee. I'll never forget that image."

"Where were you last night? In fact, where were all three of you?"

"Here. And, before you ask, no one could verify that. Look at where we are. There's not another habitation for at least a half mile from here," Wendy said.

"Did you kill your husband and his lover?"

"No."

"Did you have your friends kill him?"

"No. Don't be ridiculous."

While Nadine interviewed Wendy, she couldn't help but notice the various unfinished canvases in her studio.

"Those are interesting paintings. What does the symbolism mean?"

"Those are ancient Druid symbols, all of which have various meanings," Wendy explained.

"Why Druid?"

"I've been attracted to that belief system for many years."

"Are you and your friends planning to remain on the island for a while?" Nadine asked.

"I live here. My friends were planning to remain a week."

"I'll return to speak with them later. Now I have to contact Charlotte's husband."

"A sad duty," Wendy said.

Nadine returned to her room at the Albatross Inn, carefully avoiding engaging in any lengthy discussion with the owner Mitzi. She called Charlotte's husband: Scott Yeager.

"Mr. Yeager, I'm Detective McAfee from Maine's Major Crimes Unit. I'm sorry to tell you that your wife is dead."

"What? How?"

"She was found murdered on Moose Island, from where I'm calling you now. I've just begun the investigation."

"My god. I can't believe it."

"Your wife was found dead along with a man named Norman Manson. Do you know him?"

"The writer. I know of him."

"It appears that your wife was having an affair with him."

"What you just said is news to me. I've been separated from Charlotte for some months now. A divorce is in the works. We live in different buildings in Manhattan."

"We need you to come to Augusta to formally identify the body. Then you can plan her funeral."

"Of course. I'll make arrangements right away."

"I'll send you all of the details about how to coordinate with the state medical examiner. Once you're in Maine, we can talk more."

After Nadine ended the call, she pondered Scott Yeager's tone of voice. He had remained very calm. That in itself didn't point to any guilt. But he did have a motive if he had actually known of Charlotte's affair and had decided to do something about it. Nadine's focus was on Scott Yeager. She decided to spend the evening finding out as much about him as she could.

***

"Take a look at this," Rufus told his friends Bryant and Henry.

"Holy crap. They're dancing around naked. Look at those boobs!" Bryant said.

"But it gets better. Watch."

The boys watched enthralled as the women burned the wicker man and chanted.

"Hey, you better turn this video over to the cops. You know about the double murder last night," Henry said.

"Are you nuts? I'd be screwed if anyone found out about what I've been doing. Besides, these women had nothing to do with the murders," Rufus said.

"How do you know that?" Bryant said. "Were you there all night with them?"

"No. Of course not. I went home."

"You're in deep shit, Rufus. I'd delete that if I were you."

"Neither of you better say a fucking thing to anybody about this."

Later that night in his room, Rufus had his finger poised over the delete button, but he couldn't bring himself to erase the footage. He had become intoxicated by the images he had recorded.

16

Rufus's sister Maggie knew that something was going on with her brother and his friends, but she wasn't sure what it was. She knew that he crept out of the house at night. She knew that he often spent hours in the woods with his friends during the day. She didn't like the fact that he got away with these things when she had to stay home and practice the piano, upon the insistence of her mother.

One day, after completing her obligatory piano session with her aged teacher Miss Hawkins, she heard her brother leave the house. She followed him, but from a safe distance. From a hiding place in the woods, Rufus and his friends gathered together in a secluded section of the island, far from any of the paths that tourists hiked. The boys were drinking beer and watching a video on his phone.

From where she was hiding, she could not see what they were watching. But she suspected it was something pornographic.

She returned home and walked into her mother Samantha's graphic design studio, which was located in the attic of their house.

"I came down from my office to take a break and I found he house empty," Samantha said. "Where were you?"

"I followed Rufus and his friends. They're doing something that I don't think is right," Maggie said.

Then Maggie went on to chronicle all that she knew about Rufus's secretive activities. Samantha called her husband Phil and told him Maggie's story.

"I'll be home shortly. I'll have Shorty close up for the day," Phil said.

When Rufus walked into the house an hour later, his entire family was waiting for him in the living room

"Where have you been?" Samantha said.

"Out with my buddies."

"Let me see your phone."

"Why?"

"Give it to me, Rufus," Phil said sternly, grabbing the phone from his son's hand. Phil began watching the video.

"Jesus Christ, Rufus. Are you out of your mind? Who are these women?"

"It's the artist Wendy and some of her friends," Rufus said.

"That's the woman whose husband was murdered," Samantha said. "Why didn't you say anything? This video needs to be turned over to the police."

"I guess I didn't want to get in trouble," Rufus said.

"That ship has sailed," Phil said. "You're grounded for the rest of the summer. And this phone is impounded."

Rufus shot a vicious look at his sister, whom he suspected of spying on him. It was all Maggie could do to suppress a smile.

***

Nadine was reviewing the autopsy report on Norman and Charlotte from the medical examiner when she received a phone call from Phil Nugent, who urgently wanted her to come to his house. She couldn't believe the video when she saw it. The footage was incriminating, especially for Wendy. In addition, the forensics team had found fingerprints of an unknown third person in the cottage along with those of Norman and Charlotte. Nadine immediately trudged to Wendy's cottage.

"Explain this ceremony to me," Nadine said, showing Wendy the video.

"Where did you get this?"

"Do you know a boy named Rufus? He secretly filmed you and your friends."

"Shit," Wendy muttered.

"We found some fingerprints at the cottage. I suspect that they're yours. Let me ask you again: did you kill Norman and Charlotte in a fit of jealous rage?"

"No. But, yes, the fingerprints are probably mine. I was there on several occasions. But I didn't murder them. Whoever killed them must have had bloody clothes. You can search my cottage all you want. But you won't find anything tying me to the murders."

"You could have burned your clothes. You have a makeshift fire pit near where your friends have pitched their tents."

"Have your team sift through the ashes. You won't find any fabric there. I didn't kill them."

"But you wanted him dead. I watched the video. Your chant talked about slaying him."

"We all had too much wine by that point in the evening. It was all a joke."

"A pretty sick one," Nadine said.

Nadine made a call asking for the state forensics team to return to the island to fingerprint Wendy and her friends and thoroughly search through Wendy's cottage and property. The medical examiner had concluded that the murder weapon was likely a household butcher knife. And that the stakes pounded through the hands of the victims were made of red maple. The stakes were likely whittled to a sharp point by a common pocket knife.

Could Wendy and her friends have collectively killed Norman and Charlotte? The bodies were dragged from the bed down the stairs and into the backyard. Could Wendy have accomplished that alone? Could she have accomplished it with the help of her Druid friends? Even though Wendy had a motive, Nadine doubted that it was Wendy, who was weird but not likely a killer.

While waiting for the forensics report on Wendy's property, Nadine turned her attention to Scott Yeager. A vice president at Mutual Bank in New York, he and Charlotte had been married ten years. They had no children. Scott claimed that he was in New York on the evening that his wife was murdered. Nadine ordered the Major Crimes Unit to retrieve his cell phone records.

It was also fortunate that the dock at Stillwater Cove did have a security camera to monitor all of the tourists' parked vehicles. Nadine studied the footage, looking for Scott among the many visitors to the island. She did not spot him.

When Scott's cell phone records were delivered to Nadine, she noticed that one number in particular had been called dozens of times in the days prior to the murder. But the calls had ended after Charlotte's death. The phone number, Nadine discovered, belonged to Scott's brother Steve, who lived in the small Maine village of Otter Creek, near the border with the Canadian province of New Brunswick.

Steve Yeager had a record for drug dealing in New York City. After serving a two-year sentence, he left New York and moved to a very remote part of Maine, where he made wooden furniture. Nadine printed off a photo from Steve's website, which featured many varieties of handsome chairs and tables that he hand crafted. His look had changed over the years. He once sported long black hair in his police mug shot. Now, he had short-cropped blond hair.

Nadine walked over to the Sea Breeze hotel and asked to see the guest list from the time of the murders. There was no one named Steve Yeager who had registered. Then she showed his photo to several members of the restaurant and housekeeping staff. One of the waitresses recognized his face.

"He was a good-looking man. Rugged. With big hands. But quiet. He barely spoke when I served him," a waitress said.

"Did he tell you his name?" Nadine said.

"No. Never did."

Nadine then asked the front desk clerk about who had stayed in the room next to that of Charlotte.

"Let me see. It was a gentleman named Red Saunders. He paid cash for four nights."

Nadine showed him Steve's picture.

"Yes, that's him."

Nadine returned to her room at the Albatross Inn. She debated about what to do. If she called Scott, she ran the risk that he would alert Steve, who might flee. Was Steve acting on Scott's behalf? Had his physical appearance changed so much that his sister-in-law Charlotte hadn't spotted him on the island? That's what she needed to discover. She planned to leave Moose Island on the first ferry in the morning and drive deep into the vast north woods of Maine.

17

Nadine thought the line of towering pine trees would never end as she continued to drive north toward Otter Creek, a small hamlet of less than five hundred people. She wondered how Steve Yeager could make a living there making furniture. But then again, she figured, the internet enabled people who craved isolation to make a living conducting commerce virtually.

After seeing the highway sign indicating that Otter Creek was just five miles away, she began to notice a few modest houses scattered in the woods. Some were low-slung wood-sided abodes, whereas others were single-wide trailer homes.

Her GPS navigation directed her to turn down a dirt road before she entered the village. The road was rutted. The tall trees blocked out most of the sunlight. In the distance she spotted a sign that read "Yeager Furniture Mill." She saw a battered pickup truck parked in front of a workshop that had a small house attached.

She parked behind the truck and knocked on the door of the shop. She heard footsteps and then Yeager appeared, wearing a torn black T-shirt and jeans that were ripped at the knees.

"How can I help you?" he said.

"I'm Detective Nadine McAfee. You are Steve Yeager, brother of Scott?"

"Yes. How can I help you?"

"I'd like to talk to you about the murders of Norman Manson and your sister-in-law Charlotte."

"Yes, Scott called me about their deaths. Awful stuff. Come on in."

"How did you pick up this skill of making furniture?"

"There was an apprentice program in prison. You probably know already that I served time. I learned it there. Then, after my parole, I read about an old woodworking master who lived way up here in the Maine woods. He took me in and helped me hone my skills. The old man died about six months ago. They don't make him like that anymore."

"I know you were on Moose Island during the time of the murders. I have witnesses putting you at the Sea Breeze hotel. In fact, you stayed in the room right next to Charlotte's. You're not going to tell me you weren't there, are you?" Nadine said bluntly.

"You got me dead to rights, sheriff," Steve retorted sarcastically. "Yeah, I was there. My brother Scott wanted me to keep an eye on her. He was worried that Manson's crazy-ass wife would find out and kill them both. And that's what happened, isn't it? Why are you here when you should be talking to her?"

"I'm here talking to you, Steve."

"I didn't kill them."

"Where were you the night of the murders?"

"In my hotel room."

"You were there when the word got out about the murders. Why didn't you say anything? Why did you leave the island?"

"Because Scott didn't want anyone to find out I was spying for him. Plus, I have a record. I might be accused of the crime. Like what you're doing right now."

Nadine didn't want to engage in a rhetorical back-and-forth with him when she had no physical evidence against him. She needed to dig deeper into the arrangement he had with his brother.

"Is there any place to stay in this town? A motel or something?" Nadine said.

"Ruby Willis has a small place with a couple of rooms right in the village. She's a friend of mine. We don't get many tourists up here."

Nadine headed into town. Ruby's establishment was not hard to find. She had two dismally appointed rooms that were accessed via a set of outside stairs above her garage. Nadine was pleased that the toilet and shower functioned properly. The bed creaked. Barely any natural light entered the room. But miraculously, there was an internet connection. Even at the ends of the world people needed to stay electronically connected.

She contacted the financial forensics division, asking them to check the Yeager brothers' bank records. Nadine walked to the only diner in town where she had an uninspired meal of fried chicken and mashed potatoes. By the time she returned to her room, darkness had fallen. There was an email waiting for her. Scott Yeager had electronically transferred ten thousand dollars into his brother's bank account just two days before Charlotte's death. The coincidence was too stark to ignore. She put in a call to Captain Davies to send a team up to Otter Creek tomorrow to search Steve's property.

With nothing more to be done until morning, Nadine settled into her room. She eventually drifted off to sleep. Her slumber was interrupted abruptly at two o'clock in the morning when she heard the creaking of the wooden stairs that led to her room. She reached for her gun and sat up, her every sense on edge. She heard the sound of a key opening the door of her room. She slid off the bed, finding a space between the bed and the outside wall in which to crouch. The door opened. A slash of light from outside revealed the silhouette of a small figure.

"Stop right there!" Nadine yelled.

The figure turned and began descending the stairs. Nadine followed. She had no shoes on and wore only sweat pants and a University of Maine T-shirt. She followed the figure, which from its petite stature was likely a woman, running around the corner of the garage. Nadine turned the corner and was knocked off of her feet by a sharp blow to the head by a piece of lumber. Stunned, she managed to maintain the grip on her revolver.

"Steve, watch out. She still has her gun," the woman yelled. She recognized the voice as that of Ruby.

Steve Yeager then entered her line of sight. He approached her wielding a large knife that looked like a machete. He swung the weapon at her head. She ducked. The blade struck the side of the garage and lodged in the wood momentarily. He pulled it out and lunged toward Nadine, who fired, hitting him in the chest. The bullet did not stop his momentum forward, however. He fell on the ground next to Nadine, blood draining out of his wound.

Nadine breathed heavily. Looking up, she then saw Ruby approaching. Ruby reached down to grab the machete. Nadine pointed the gun at her, telling her not to move.

"What's going on here?" a man said. He appeared suddenly from the shadows, pointing a shotgun at Nadine.

"Lower your gun. I'm a police officer making an arrest of this woman."

"Ruby, is that you? What's going on? Is that Steve lying there?"

"Frank, just do as she says. Steve's dead. Don't get yourself shot, too."

"Who are you?" Nadine asked.

"I'm Frank Bower. I live above the hardware store next door."

"Frank, I'm Detective McAfee. Put your gun down and go back and call 911. Do it now!"

After Bower departed, Nadine looked toward Ruby, who lay on the ground with her hands intertwined behind her head.

"What do you think you would have accomplished by killing me?" Nadine said.

"We were going to make it look like you were just disappeared. We were going to burn you and your car deep in the woods," Ruby confessed. "No one would ever find you."

"A pretty dumb plan by a pair of dumb shits," Nadine snorted. "What's your relationship with Steve?"

"We're a couple I guess," Ruby said.

"I hope he was worth it."

"No man is worth this."

***

"Are you feeling better, Grandma?" Nadine said after returning home.

"Much better. But I told you I would be fine," Martha said. "It's a shame what happened to those people on the island."

"The brother Scott was charged with orchestrating the murders to implicate Wendy Wiseman," Nadine said. "But the real killer was his brother Steve, who is now dead."

"So much jealousy in the world. And for what?

"Good question."

"Will the widow remain on the island?"

"That's what I heard. She loves it there. She plans to stay. After I gave her the details about the plot to frame her for murder, she told me that she felt a spiritual connection with the island," Nadine said. "Grief was not an emotion that she wanted to hold on to."

"She sounds like a wise woman."

"Maybe the wisest of them all."

PART 3: SIBLING RIVALRY

18

"You won't believe this, Grandma," Nadine said. "But some of Duke's friends bailed him out after he was charged with burglary. Now, apparently, he has joined some underground militia that's preparing for a second civil war. He's moved to this armed camp up near the border with Quebec."

"Duke was so stable and normal when you were married to him," Martha said. "Now, he's turned into a gun nut with grievances against everybody. I just don't understand it."

"Too much right-wing cable news and talk radio," Nadine said. "I even know some people on the force who sympathize with some of these far-out views. In fact, more than one person told me that it's the liberals who come here from Boston and New York who are causing all of the problems. A fellow officer thinks Maine should secede from the United States."

"People are pitting one person against another, like a giant family squabble," Martha sighed.

"And when squabbles get out of hand, somebody usually gets injured or killed. I worry about being caught in the middle of somebody's grievances that turn deadly."

"I don't envy your job, Nadine," Martha said. "But the good news is that the apple pie that I baked should be ready now."

***

Mitzi Fairhaven, the owner of the Albatross Inn, looked at the clock in the small dining room where her guests and the occasional island resident were served breakfast each morning. It read one minute before eight o'clock in the morning. When retired lobsterman and widower Sam Leary walked in, she knew that it would be exactly eight o'clock.

Ever since Sam's wife of forty years Ella died two years ago, Sam punctually visited Mitzi's inn to have breakfast and to chat with her. Twice divorced with her gray hair pulled back from the leathery skin on her face, Mitzi loved to talk. That's why she opened the inn in the first place. She loved to talk to the hundreds of strangers who stayed at her establishment from all over the world. But Sam was different. He was a local, born and bred on the island as was his father and grandfather. With large hands and a face raw from decades at sea, he was the definition of an old sea salt. But, Mitzi thought, he was a kind and generous man who always looked out for his fellow islanders. If a storm damaged a house, he was the first one there with his tools to help repair it. If there was an accident at sea, his boat was the first out searching for the missing person.

He lived in the same tidy two-story house near the center of the island where he and his now deceased wife raised their three daughters, all of whom left the island seeking a more comfortable lifestyle. Even though Sam lived modestly, Mitzi and other long-timers on the island all had heard the rumors that he was very wealthy. And that he had earned hundreds of thousands of dollars through savvy land investments.

"Looks like we'll have a bit of rain this afternoon," Sam said. Mitzi personally brought him his usual breakfast of two slices of wheat toast, scrambled eggs, and strong black coffee.

"That's good to hear. The weather has been drier and hotter than normal this autumn," Mitzi observed.

"Have you met that artist whose husband was killed?" Sam said.

"Oh, yes. That purple hair is a sight to see. The detective who solved the case stayed with me. A nice woman. She lives with her grandmother on the mainland. She's divorced. Don't know why she never married. She's an attractive young woman," Mitzi said, revealing how much information she was able to glean about Nadine's life in the short time Nadine had stayed with her.

"Some people just aren't wired to be married."

"Are you talking about me, Sam Leary?"

"No. I'm talking about my three daughters. Two of them had or still have a troubled marriage, or so I hear, and the third daughter Gwen never married.

"You told me that Karen was having marriage issues. You mean Regina also broke up with her husband?"

"Yeah. His name's Ed. A good-for-nothing son-of-a-bitch if you ask me. He played football at the state university, but then he became an auto mechanic who jumped from job to job for years. Regina told me that he also drank and gambled."

"You wonder what she saw in him in the first place," Mitzi mused. "Did you and Ella try to warn her?"

"We kept out of their private business. We figured our job was done when they left the island to make their own way in the world. They are adults. Let them figure it out, god damnit," Sam said, his voice rising.

"Don't let it bother you," Mitzi said.

"What bothers me is that Regina wants to return to the island and stay with me for a while until things cool down in the divorce proceedings. Jesus Christ, the woman is in her mid-thirties and she wants to live with her old man. That's pathetic, if you ask me."

"But are you going to let her stay here?"

"I guess so. What am I going to do? Tell her to get lost? I can't do that. I can still hear Ella's voice in my head telling me to be understanding."

"When does she arrive?"

"On tomorrow's morning ferry."

"Bring her over here. I haven't seen her since he was a teenager."

"Sure. The more you talk with her the less I have to. I have my daily routine and she's going to fuck it all up," Sam said.

Sam finished his breakfast and waved goodbye to Mitzi. He returned home and turned on his computer. Since he retired, he vowed not to become one of those old farts who lived in the past, hankering for the return of typewriters and rotary phones. He leapt feet-first into the internet age. He also bought a smartphone. He downloaded books to read and worked on the *New York Times* crossword puzzle online each morning. But now his middle daughter was returning. After completing the puzzle, he walked upstairs to Regina's old room and made sure the bed had fresh sheets. He then dusted the room. He always liked to be neat.

***

In a small house near the edge of Portland, Maine, Regina stuffed clothes and toiletries into a large black duffel bag. Her older sister Karen had stopped by after learning that she was headed back to Moose Island.

"I'm sorry to hear about you and Ed," Karen said.

"Shit happens," Regina said.

"Things may be heading in the same direction for me and Mike."

"Really?"

"I think he's been seeing one of his coworkers at the law firm. But I have no proof."

"Asshole."

"Have you ever thought what your life is going to be like when you're fifty or sixty?" Karen said. "Do you think you'll have enough money? Or will you be living in some shitty apartment or, worse yet, in a fucking trailer park?"

"I don't know. I never thought about it much."

"Well. You should. I know I have," Karen said. "Do you think dad is rich?"

"I don't know."

"When mom was alive, she told me once that dad invested well when he was younger. In oceanside real-estate and stuff like that. She told me that we would be taken care of when he died."

"Well, dad's not dead. He'll probably live to be one hundred. He'll outlive us and we won't see a dime," Regina said. "He'd probably do it to spite us."

"How did he take the fact that you want to stay with him for a while?"

"He grumbled but eventually agreed."

"Tell him I said hello. Maybe I'll come and visit. And maybe I can even convince Gwen to spend a weekend with us."

"He always liked Gwen the best. She's the wunderkind who went and got her doctorate and now is a big fucking ivy league biomedical professor."

"Just try not to get the old man wound up," Karen said.

"I'll be the dutiful daughter," Regina said.

"That in itself will shock dad," Karen laughed.

19

When Regina walked into her old room, she felt a wave of nostalgia and embarrassment wash over her. Nostalgia for the warm memories of growing up in this house on a far-flung Maine island. Embarrassment for having to return as a grown woman.

Her father met her at the ferry dock. To Regina, he seemed to walk slower than she had remembered. And his posture now resembled a question mark. Like all children of aging parents, she wondered how many years he had left to live. And whether he would die quickly or suffer through a protracted illness.

Now, however, Regina's major concern was her personal finances. Her working career, such as it was, consisted of low remuneration jobs starting from the time she had left the island. After graduating from high school, she moved to Portland, where she worked as a waitress. Then she found a job as a front desk clerk at a motel. It was during this time that she met her soon-to-be-ex-husband Ed. After leaving the front desk position, she worked at a rental car agency at the Portland airport. The jobs had no benefits. And they were mind-numbing. Now, at the age of thirty-five, Regina found her prospects dim and her bank account meagre. She was thankful for her early decision in her marriage to put off having children because she and Ed could barely support themselves, much less a family. Her father now was the only financial lifeline she had.

After settling into her old room, she went downstairs and offered to make lunch for her father.

"How long do you plan on staying here?" Sam said.

"I don't know. I just arrived. Are you ready to get rid of me already?"

"No. It's just that since your mother passed, I've become used to living alone. I have my own routine. You living here was not part of my retirement plans," he said.

"I'll give you your space, if that is what you're asking."

"That would be preferable. Now that you've returned, you can spend time exploring the island again."

"It's a small island. After a week, I would have covered every inch," Regina said.

"You can use that week to plan your next move," Sam said. "You do have a job back in Portland, don't you?"

"Yes, but not a very good one."

"You should have gone to college like your sister Gwen. Karen made the same mistake as you. You can't get ahead in the world without a college education."

"You did all right for yourself," Regina snapped back.

"Different times. Different times," Sam retorted. "Look, this old lobsterman isn't living in the past. Notice the computer? Here's my iPhone."

"Yes, you've become very modern."

"How are your finances?"

"Bleak."

"Maybe you could enroll in community college or something like that. Learn a marketable skill."

"I'll think about that," Regina said.

Her anger and frustration were welling up inside her, and she had only been back to Moose Island for a few hours.

Sam told her that he was going to settle into his crossword puzzle, followed by reading, and then his afternoon nap.

Since the weather was pleasant, Regina did leave the house. She walked to the northern tip of the island. She knew the paths like a local. She eventually came to a rocky lookout that plunged to the ocean. She recalled spending time here with her sister Karen. The two of them were only two years apart and have always had a sisterly bond. Gwen was five years younger. Neither one felt especially close to Gwen, who forged her own high-profile academic path.

Regina called Karen from her lofty perch.

"How's it going back at the homestead?" Karen said.

"Dad seems perturbed that I'm back here. He already asked me how long I would be staying."

"Sounds like dad."

"Do you know anything about his will?"

"What do you mean?"

"I mean do you know how much money he has and who will get it? Did he ever talk about it with you?"

"No," Karen said. "But I assume now that mother is dead that his estate will be divided among the three of us."

"Do you know for sure?"

"No. Why are you bringing this up?"

"I don't have any money, Karen. I have a few hundred dollars in a savings account. That's it. What about you? Are you financially secure?"

"If Mike leaves me, I'll have nothing. He's the one with the income," Karen said.

"How did we get ourselves into this position?" Regina wondered.

"The question now is: how do we get out of it?" Karen said. "I have some ideas. Let me call dad. I'll tell him that I'd like to stay a few days and keep him company."

"You were always the schemer," Regina said.

"But now the stakes are higher."

20

Sam was surprised and perturbed when Regina told him that Karen was planning to come to the island to visit. The last time Karen set foot on Moose Island was two years ago for her mother's funeral. Now suddenly Karen felt a need to come all the way from Portland to visit him and his sister, Sam thought. Not that he didn't love his children. He did. But he also relished his independence and privacy, which were both compromised by having two of his three daughters circling around him.

"Why is Karen coming?" Sam said. "Doesn't she still have her job at the L.L. Bean store?"

"Yes. But she's taking time off," Regina said. "Plus, she and Mike are having some issues."

"Jesus Christ," Sam exclaimed. "Is she going to get divorced too?"

"Maybe. She's not sure. But it might be heading that way."

"And suddenly my house has become a refuge for the imminently divorced?"

"You don't have to be so sarcastic. Karen and I are going through a tough time. You could show some empathy."

"I spent most of my adult life going out to sea every morning in all types of weather to raise you three girls. I thought Ella and I taught you to stand on your own two feet. Doesn't sound like you were paying much attention to that lesson."

"Times are tough now."

"They've always been tough. Don't give me that bullshit."

Regina knew that she could never win an argument with Sam when he got himself fired up with righteous indignation. She looked at her watch. It was time to head to the ferry dock to meet Karen.

"You want to walk with me to meet Karen?"

"She knows the way. I'm going to stroll around the island by myself. I'll meet you back here," Sam said.

"Suit yourself."

Sam made a stop first at the Albatross Inn to say hello to Mitzi.

"Where have you been these last few days?" Mitzi enquired.

"Regina is here. She insists on having breakfast with me at the house. Karen is arriving this morning. My daily routine is all messed up."

"I hope to see you again when they leave. I can set my watch to your schedule."

"I'll be back. I hope sooner rather than later."

Sam continued his walk. He decided to introduce himself to the eccentric artist that everyone was talking about. He plowed through the forest, which was beginning to wear its autumn garments.

He found her cottage tucked deep into the woods. He was impressed with how she had renovated it.

He stood outside and yelled to see if anyone was home. He was greeted by a flash of purple hair.

"Good morning," Wendy said cheerfully.

"Good morning," Sam said. "I'm Sam Leary. One of the old timers here. I just wanted to welcome you to the island, although belatedly."

"That's very kind of you."

"I heard about what happened to your husband. A nasty business. Never seen the likes of it here."

"Life goes on."

"You decided to stay."

"Yes, I did. I love it here," she said. "And you do what, Sam?"

"Oh, I'm retired from decades of lobstering."

"A tough way to make a living. I just splash a bunch of paint colors on canvas."

"We all have a role to play," Sam said. "I'll leave you to it. I have to get back. Two of my three daughters suddenly decided to visit."

"You don't sound happy about it."

"They seem to think that I can help them solve their personal and financial issues."

"And can you?"

"That's not my job."

"When I hear stories like that, I'm glad I never had children."

"Stick to painting," Sam said with a wry smile on his face.

Sam meandered his way across the island and back to his house, where he found Karen and Regina talking in the kitchen. They were having tea, a beverage that Sam abhorred. He didn't even like the aroma. He was a black coffee man.

"Hi, Dad," Karen said. She knew not to rise and hug him. He was not that kind of a father.

"Hello," Sam mumbled.

"Come join us," Karen said.

Sam sat down at the table and poured himself a cup of his favorite hearty Colombian brew.

"I hear that you and Mike might get divorced. Is that true?"

"Maybe. Things just haven't worked out."

"I see," Sam said. "So, how long do you plan on staying here?"

"I'm not sure yet," Karen said. "It's beautiful on the island this time of year. Most of the tourists are gone. The island is for islanders again."

"Dad," Regina said. "Karen and I have been talking. Now don't get mad when I say this. But we were wondering if you would tell us about your estate plans. As your daughters, we have a right to know things. Like, for example, who is the executor of your will?"

"So, this is what this family pow-wow is all about. I notice that there is one daughter missing. Should I expect Gwen to walk through that door any minute?"

"No," Karen said. "She doesn't even know we are here."

"If you must know," Sam said. "I have given the power of attorney to my friend Walt Bouvier in Stillwater Cove."

"Why him?"

"Because we've been friends for forty years and I trust him," Sam explained. "And if you're really wondering how much money I have and who's going to get it, you'll have to wait until I'm dead. But don't let the suspense kill you," Sam said, rising from the kitchen table.

"That went really fucking well, Karen," Regina said.

"We had to get it out in the open," Karen said. "Besides, I have a plan. Let's go upstairs and chat. It'll be just like old times."

Sam could hear his daughters climbing the stairs to their respective rooms. He felt as if the vultures were circling.

21

After Karen and Regina had raised the issue of his will, Sam tried to keep his distance from his daughters. But this was difficult since they occupied their childhood bedrooms. Even though they remained in his home, Sam began again to have his breakfast each morning at Mitzi's inn.

"How are things on the home front?" Mitzi said.

"My daughters suddenly are showing an interest in both my health and finances," Sam replied. "Fortunately, both are in fine condition."

Sam returned home and went about his normal routine, ignoring his daughters' presence as much as possible. But

Regina and Karen insisted that the three of them enjoy dinner outside since it was a warm autumn evening.

"We won't get many more nights like this," Karen said.

"Dad, if you grill some steaks, Karen and I will prepare the salad."

The daughters avoided the contentious issue of money. Instead, they shared memories of their late mother and news of their sister Gwen's latest research into infectious diseases.

"Gwen told me that the federal government has hired her as a consultant to work on identifying how rare diseases can be passed from animals to humans," Sam said. "She now travels to Washington once a month."

"Any signs that she'll ever get married?" Regina said.

"She's married to her work," Karen said.

After dinner Sam remained on the porch while his daughters cleared the able. He suddenly began to tremble even though it was still unseasonably warm. He tried to arise from his chair but felt dizzy. Then his body became convulsed with nausea. He shuffled to a row of nearby bushes and vomited.

"What's wrong, Dad?" Regina asked.

"I don't know. I suddenly felt ill. It feels like food poisoning. Do you feel OK?" Sam said.

"Yes. I feel fine. Karen, are you feeling ill?"

"No."

"Let me help you back into the house," Regina said.

Sam reclined on the sofa. After about an hour his headache and nausea had passed.

"I think I'm going to take some aspirin and retire for the evening," he said.

The following morning Sam still didn't feel quite right. He was unsteady coming down the stairs from his bedroom. Karen insisted that he not walk to the Albatross Inn this morning.

"We'll make you breakfast," Karen said.

After finishing his meal, Sam decided to go for a walk, saying that he needed the fresh air to clear his head. His joints ached. He feared that he may be developing arthritis or some other muscular malady. Even though he was sixty-five, he had never felt old. Not until the past twenty-four hours.

Just a few minutes into his walk, however, he feel the muscles in his legs convulse. His heart began to race. He knew enough to understand the signs of an impending heart attack. He turned around, but quickly fell to the ground. He inhaled the aroma of the pine forest before he lost consciousness.

That morning Wendy Wiseman was heading to the general store to pick up her supply of art materials that she had ordered from the mainland. She discovered Sam's body lying in the path. She shook him, but he did not move. She ran to his house and informed his daughters about what had happened. Regina and Karen ran to the spot where Sam lay.

"I think he's dead," Regina said.

"I'll call 911," Karen said.

***

At the funeral home in Stillwater Cove, Gwen Leary stood in front of her two sisters, trying to understand the circumstances surrounding her father's sudden death.

"The man was as strong as a bull," Gwen said. "I just don't understand how he could drop dead of a heart attack."

"It happens all of the time. Even marathon runners who are in great shape suddenly die," Regina said. "You're a scientist. You must know that it could happen to anyone."

"But we never expect it to happen to someone we know," Gwen said.

"We never do," Karen said.

Sam Leary's body was transported in a coffin on a ferry back to Moose Island to be buried next to Ella. A cold rain fell during the graveside ceremony, which drew most of the year-round island residents.

That evening, after the mourners had all departed, having delivered their condolences, Gwen, Regina, and Karen sat in their childhood home sharing a bottle of wine.

"It feels weird to be back here again under these circumstances," Gwen said.

"Don't forget that we have an appointment with Walt Bouvier tomorrow at ten o'clock for the reading of dad's will," Regina said.

"Other than this house, I don't expect it will be very substantial," Gwen said.

"You'd be surprised," Karen said.

"What do you mean?"

"The rumors are that dad made several savvy real-estate deals in his life that netted him some serious money."

"Oh, come on. Dad a real-estate baron?"

"He was more than your typical laconic Maine lobsterman," Regina chimed in.

***

Walt Bouvier's cramped legal office sat above a tiny grocery store in Stillwater Cove. The room was musty and damp. He greeted the daughters warmly, expressing his shock that Sam should have died so suddenly.

"Well, let's get right to it. That's what Sam would have wanted," Walt said.

Walt went on to explain that after Ella died, Sam had amended his will to its present wording.

"I think you girls will be pleasantly surprised at how well he took care of you," he said.

Walt then revealed that the total value of Sam's estate, in cash and property, was one million, two hundred thousand dollars, to be equally distributed among the three daughters.

"Now, understand that the bulk of the estate lies in the value of the house and the surrounding land, which has appreciated considerably since you were children. You'll have to decide if you want to keep the house or sell it and split the proceeds," he explained.

"I can't believe this," Gwen said.

Regina and Karen looked at each other, trying to suppress their glee.

On the ferry back to the island, Karen wondered aloud who they should select as their real-estate agent to help with the sale of the house.

"Wait a minute. We just buried dad yesterday and you want to talk about selling the house?" Gwen said. "Maybe we should keep it."

"What would be the point of that?" Karen said. "None of us plans to live here. We all have lives on the mainland."

"Maybe I want to spend time here as a getaway," Gwen said. "I think we should consider keeping it in the family."

"Do you know what property on Moose Island is worth these days?" Regina said. "Our old house is a gold mine."

"Let's not be too hasty. That's all I'm saying."

This was not how Karen had envisioned for things to turn out. Gwen was always the outlier. Always doing something to overshadow her two older sisters. Gwen's sudden nostalgia for island life irritated Karen, who decided she needed to consult Regina about their next steps to secure their future.

22

"Why do you want to live here, Gwen?" Karen asked bluntly. "Help me understand why you suddenly have this affection for the island when you went all across the country to go to college at Stanford?"

"But I came back to New England for my graduate studies. And I now teach in Boston. I'm still drawn to the area," Gwen said.

"Here's the deal, Gwen," Regina said. "Karen and I are going through some tough times with our marriages. And we're thinking about our future. We want to be more self-sufficient. We don't have the luxury of living in a gracious Boston townhouse while earning a six-figure salary."

"So, selling the house is all about your financial well-being?"

"That's right. And you want to deny us that because of some phony nostalgia that you have." Karen said.

"It's not phony."

"Let's quit arguing and take a deep breath," Regina said. "The weather is fine today. Let's go to the cliffs on the north end of the island and have a picnic. Then we can discuss this matter rationally. And maybe work out an acceptable compromise."

"I never expected you to be the voice of reason," Gwen said.

"Sometimes I can surprise you."

The daughters prepared lunch and stuffed it into several small coolers, which they carried to a scenic cliff that offered a magnificent view of the Atlantic stretching out to the horizon.

"The sea looks almost like glass today," Gwen said. "It's so calm."

"Remember when we were girls?" Regina said. "We used to creep close to the edge with our arms outstretched, close our eyes, and pretend to fly."

"I remember," Gwen said.

Regina rose from the blanket that had been spread on the rocks and walked to the edge of the cliff.

"Come on, you two," she said.

Gwen and Karen followed. They all stretched out their arms and arched their backs, as if prepared to soar to the heavens. With a swift move, Regina pushed Gwen off the cliff. Gwen let out a clipped scream before she plunged to the rocks below. Karen looked down at her younger sister's twisted, unmoving body.

"What a tragedy," Karen said coldly.

"Gwen was so clumsy at times. She stood too close to the edge and lost her footing," Regina said. "You're the best at sounding hysterical. You make the emergency call."

***

"Nadine," said Captain Davies. "I just received a call from a woman in Boston who claims to be the partner of Gwen Leary. She said she'd like to talk to a detective about Ms. Leary's death."

"And who is Gwen Leary?" Nadine said.

"She died a week ago in a fall on Moose Island. The woman, Vivian Acosta, is a physician at Mass General

Hospital. She has doubts about the nature of Ms. Leary's death."

"Oh, yes. I remember the incident now. The cause of death was determined to be from severe internal injuries consistent with a fall," Nadine said. "So, why is this woman suspicious?"

"She says she has information that she'd like to share. I'd like you to look into it. Talk to her. Here's her cell number."

"OK," Nadine said.

Not considering the matter urgent, Nadine continued with her task of clearing the yard of leaves while her grandmother Martha prepared dinner for the two of them.

Later that evening, Nadine made the call to Dr. Acosta.

"Dr. Acosta, this is Detective McAfee from Maine's Major Crimes Unit. How can I help you?"

"Thanks for calling. I was a friend to Gwen. No, let me rephrase that. We were romantically involved and were planning to move in together," Vivian said. "I don't believe her death was an accident."

"I don't mean to be insensitive, but are you letting your grief get the best of you? All evidence at the time pointed to a tragic accident. I read her sisters' statements. They said Gwen slipped and fell. About one to two people a year die on those cliffs," Nadine said. "Unfortunately, it happens."

"I think one of the sisters deliberately killed her. Moreover, Gwen thinks that her sisters may have killed their father. She sent me a series of text messages the night before she died. I'll forward them to you."

"Yes, please forward them. I'll review them and decide whether a further investigation is warranted," Nadine said.

After reading the text messages from Gwen and beginning to comprehend the family dynamics that may have been in play, Nadine could understand how Vivian Acosta could be suspicious of the sisters' account of Gwen's death.

"I received some text messages that Gwen had sent Dr. Acosta," Nadine said to Captain Davies. "I also read the sisters' statements about their father's symptoms before he collapsed. Gwen wasn't convinced that her father died of a heart attack."

"Isn't that what the autopsy proved?"

"Yes, but something may have been missed."

"What are you suggesting?"

"That we get a court order to have Sam Leary's body exhumed so another post-mortem examination can be performed."

"I'll work on securing that order. But you need to return to Moose Island and talk to the surviving sisters. If you think there's something more than meets the eye, let me know," Davies said.

"Maybe I should buy a house on the island since I have been spending so much time there."

"There are worse places to be."

Nadine made arrangements to return to Moose Island and stay at the Albatross Inn. She couldn't wait to hear Mitzi's take on the situation.

23

"When does Sybil think she'll have the listing ready to go?" Regina asked Karen. Regina was referring to Sybil Jennings, their real-estate agent.

"She's coming from the mainland today to take photos. She said she was even going to bring a drone to take some aerial footage. The listing should be up in a day or two," Karen said.

Since the deaths of their father and sister, Karen and Regina had been cleaning the family home and minimizing the clutter to try to make the house a showpiece of island serenity for potential buyers.

While they were busy with last-minute preparations, they received an unexpected visit from Mitzi.

"This is a surprise, Mitzi," Regina said. "What brings you here this morning?"

"You should know that you've drawn the attention of the police. Namely, Detective Nadine McAfee, who's planning to arrive on the ferry later this morning," Mitzi said.

"And you know this how?"

"Because she's booked a room at my inn," Mitzi said. "Why would the police be coming here? Does it have something to do with Sam's death? I can't reconcile myself to how he died."

"Don't let your grief put strange thoughts in your head. I know he was your friend. But dad died of a heart attack. I'm sure the detective's visit is just routine."

"Well, I just think it's strange. I wanted you to know."

Regina shot a worrisome look at Karen after Mitzi had departed.

"Did we miss something?" Regina said. "Why would a detective suddenly be coming? The deaths were not considered suspicious."

"I don't know. But we'll be interviewed by this detective. You can bet on that. We have to be calm and smart. Stick to our story," Karen said. "Let's just keep our minds focused on the house sale."

***

It felt like a homecoming when Nadine checked into her room at the Albatross Inn. Mitzi greeted her like an old friend. The refreshing aroma of the island invigorated Nadine's senses as she walked to Sam Leary's house. She carried a court order to exhume his body from the island's cemetery.

"Good morning, I'm Detective McAfee," she announced while handing over the court order to Karen.

"What's this?" Karen said.

"An order to exhume your father's body so the medical examiner can conduct a more thorough autopsy."

"Wait just a minute. Why is this necessary? Why are you even here?"

"I believe you met a Dr. Vivian Acosta at Gwen's memorial service in Boston?"

"Yes. My sister and I were quite surprised that Gwen was in a romantic relationship with her," Regina said. "She never talked much about her personal life, at least not to us."

"That's surprising given you are all sisters," Nadine said.

"Gwen went her own way," Karen said. "But what were you saying about Acosta?"

"She forwarded to me a series of text messages in which Gwen confided to her that she didn't think your father died from a heart attack. And then a day after sending these messages, Gwen died in a fall. Too much of a coincidence. That's why I'm here."

"I hope you don't go in for conspiracy theories," Karen said.

"I go where the facts lead me. If the autopsy confirms a heart attack, then I can go home," Nadine said. "Now, tell me about that day on the cliffs."

"There's nothing much to tell," Regina said. "We were there having a picnic. Gwen walked too close to the edge. She lost her balance and fell. It all happened in an instant."

"I'd like to see the exact spot where she fell."

"Sure. I can take you there."

"I prefer to examine the area by myself," Nadine said.

"Suit yourself."

Nadine followed Regina's direction to the windswept promontory. A beautiful spot, Nadine said to herself after she arrived. The weather on the day Gwen fell was dry with a light breeze under five miles an hour, Nadine confirmed. So, the chances were low of her slipping on wet rocks or being blown over by a sudden gust of wind. Plus, Nadine thought, Gwen had spent her entire life on the island scrambling over these very same rocks. Although she had no way to prove it, she felt in her gut that Gwen as likely pushed deliberately to her death.

Nadine began walking back to the Albatross Inn to meet the forensics team that would exhume Leary's body and take it to Augusta for examination. Along the way, she met Wendy Wiseman gathering pine cones that had fallen to the ground.

"Detective McAfee. I didn't expect to see you again," Wendy said.

"I've been called to follow up on something."

"About Sam Leary?"

"How did you know?"

"Well, Sam visited me in the woods shortly before he died. He appeared hearty and vigorous to me. Then I was the person who discovered his body the very next day. I was quite shocked."

"What did you talk about?"

"Not much. Although he was annoyed that his daughters wanted him to solve their financial issues."

"I see," Nadine said. "Nice chatting with you again. But I have to head to the dock."

Nadine couldn't get out of her mind Wendy's comment about the apparent real reason for the daughters' return to the island. If they were hard up for money and their father would not help them, could they have been so desperate as to kill their father without being detected? Nadine hoped that the autopsy would lead her to an answer.

24

Before Nadine had even heard back from the medical examiner, she received a visit from Karen at the Albatross Inn. Nadine suggested that the pair go for a walk instead of remaining in the small dining room where Mitzi could, and probably would, overhear their conversation.

"This is a very hard thing for me to do," Karen said. "But I haven't been able to sleep at night. And I'm afraid for my own life."

"What are you talking about, Karen?"

"I know what the autopsy on my father will reveal: that he died from being poisoned by hemlock," Karen confessed.

"Poisoned?" Nadine said. "Are you confessing to killing your father?"

"No, not me. Regina. She killed him. She also killed Gwen."

"Was this all planned by you and Regina?"

"Sort of. I mean we were both desperate for money. Regina was getting divorced and I was heading that way. We heard rumors that dad had money, but he would never talk about it. Regina came here initially, hoping to convince dad to give her some money. When he wouldn't, she called me. We talked about how our lives might change after he died. Then she asked me to find some hemlock plants and bring them to the island. I did what she asked, but then I felt guilty about it. I know this sounds awful. But we were desperate. Now, I can't tolerate keeping the lie about what happened any longer."

"Tell me more about how this plot unfolded."

"I didn't want to do anything to harm dad. But apparently Regina had other ideas. I begged her not to. I didn't think she would go ahead and do it. But she did put hemlock in his food and drinks without my knowledge. It wasn't long before dad became seriously ill and then died."

"Why didn't you notify the police then, if you suspected your sister of murder?"

"I was scared for my own life. Regina threatened to kill me if I said anything," Karen said.

"What about Gwen?"

"After the funeral, we learned about how wealthy dad really was. Regina wanted to sell the family home and split the proceeds. Gwen balked. I guess that's when Regina hatched her plan to kill Gwen."

"But you would also benefit if there was one less sibling alive to get the money, correct?" Nadine observed.

"Yes, I guess so. But I never intended to harm Gwen. She's my sister. My blood. I couldn't do that."

"But Regina could?"

"She could. And she did. I was there at the cliff. She deliberately pushed Gwen to her death," Karen said.

"Yet you said nothing until now."

"Like I said. I was scared. I am scared. I can't stay on this island now that I have told you this story. Regina will kill me."

"Is this just a convenient story to hide your culpability, Karen?"

"It's the truth. Regina is a murderer. I will testify to it in court."

Nadine didn't know what to make of Karen's spontaneous confession. It would be her word against

Regina's. With little or no physical evidence available to prove which sister was the actual killer, the district attorney would have a difficult time bringing charges.

Nadine told Karen to stay at the Albatross Inn and not to return to the family home. Nadine then called Captain Davies and filled him in on what she had learned.

"Go arrest Regina Leary," Davies said. "Let the lawyers figure out what to do next."

***

"When will winter ever end?" Martha said to Nadine six months after Regina Leary had been arrested for killing her father and sister.

"It always does," Nadine said. "You'll be back in your garden before you know it."

During the frigid Maine winter, the entire state had been captivated by the legal battle between Regina and Karen. The state had formally charged Regina with two murders. Their star witness was Karen, who told the jury all about her sister's evil machinations. At several points during Karen's testimony, Regina had to be restrained from leaping from her chair and attacking Karen. Regina's defense tried to cast the blame on Karen. It came down to which sister was most believable. In the end, Regina was convicted, but her lawyers immediately appealed. Nadine knew that the court fight could last years.

From her contacts on Moose Island, Nadine learned that Karen wasted little time after the conviction of her sister to sell the family home to a wealthy family from Boston. Karen's lawyers had successfully argued that Regina was not entitled to any of her late father's estate since she was responsible for his death. Karen was now a millionaire.

***

"I have to give you credit, Karen," said her husband Mike, with whom she had now reconciled. "You really pulled it off.

"I wasn't going to let my two younger sisters have any of dad's money. As the oldest, I deserved all of it," Karen said.

"We should close on the house in Seal Harbor next week," Mike said. "I can't wait to spend our summers there. I understand that Oprah Winfrey and Martha Stewart own homes nearby."

"We're really moving up in the world."

"Let's toast to a game well played," Mike said.

William Graham

PART 4: BLOOD WEDDING

25

Senator Lindsey Beasly had booked all fifty rooms at the Sea Breeze hotel for his daughter Logan's wedding that was scheduled for Memorial Day weekend. Logan had met her future husband, Steve Bigelow, while working with him as a researcher at the Liberty Foundation, a think tank dedicated to promoting freedom from governmental intrusion into an individual's rights.

Against her father's objections, Logan had picked Moose Island for her wedding. The island was where Steve had proposed to her during a sunset sailing cruise one year earlier. The senator wondered why his daughter hadn't picked the family's Mississippi homestead, which dated back to the Civil War era.

"Most of our college friends are from the Washington, D.C. and New York region since we all went to Georgetown," Logan reminded her father. "So, traveling to Maine will be easier for them. Plus, Steve and I have a special connection to the place."

Senator Beasly wondered if he should invite his liberal senate colleagues from Maine to the ceremony as a courtesy. But he ultimately decided against it, preferring to be surrounded only by the Congressional delegation from Mississippi. He felt more comfortable around them, both personally and ideologically.

The wedding date was bittersweet for Logan, whose mother died of cancer on Memorial Day two years earlier. But she and Steve determined that enough time had passed to begin their lives together. They made sure, however, that there would be a brief tribute to the late Sara Beasly at the wedding reception, as most of the guests had met her at some point in the past.

Logan didn't care if the tribute would make uncomfortable her father's new girlfriend Heather Gilford, a TV news anchor from Jackson, Mississippi, who was thirty years younger than her father. When the pair confirmed their relationship, they became gossip fodder for the media in Mississippi and Washington, D.C. Jokes about the senator robbing the cradle made the rounds in the halls of Congress. But the senator was pleased to be seen escorting a real southern belle on his arm, and a former Miss Mississippi to boot. He knew that power was very attractive to the opposite sex.

Since Steve had introduced Logan to the pleasure of sailing early in their relationship, they agreed that their wedding would have a nautical theme. At each table would be a souvenir miniature sailboat with their respective names stenciled on the hull along with the wedding date. The night before the ceremony, the immediate family and the wedding party would dine on the deck of the yacht that Steve had booked for the occasion. His family came from a respected and wealthy family in Maryland that spent most of their summers in Maine.

The weather forecast for the weekend looked promising, albeit a bit cool. After all, it was still Maine in the spring. If the weather turned poor, the bride and groom were prepared to move the ceremony inside the Sea Breeze's main dining hall instead of the lawn that sloped down to the ocean. A perfectionist, Logan oversaw every aspect of the ceremony, down to the way the napkins were folded to look like sails.

She and Steve wanted the ceremony to be intimate and private, which is another reason they chose Moose Island. The one thing that Logan couldn't control, however, was who her father had invited to the wedding. She was fine with the state delegation, many of whom she had known since she was a child. But she chafed when she saw the name of Howard Cohen, who owned the grocery store tabloid *The Lookingglass* and several hundred local TV stations, including the one for which Heather Gilford worked.

"Why did you invite him, Dad?" Logan said.

"I've known him for thirty years. Plus, he's been a major donor to my campaigns. I couldn't say no to him."

"But he's sleazy. He publishes the most disgusting articles."

"A man has to make a living. He's no better or no worse than the lying liberal media."

"Whatever the truth is, I don't want him making a scene," Logan demanded.

"Don't worry. I'll have a chat with him when he arrives. He's a grown man. He knows how to behave," the senator said.

***

"Where the fuck is Moose Island?" Cohen said to his administrative assistant Monica.

"It's off the coast of Maine."

"Why the senator's daughter had to get married there I'll never know. Will we have some reporters embedded there?"

"Yes. I made sure that two of our staff are booked there at a small bed-and-breakfast to snoop around and take some photos in secret. It'll be a good scoop for the next edition."

"Good. Good. Now how do I get to this place?

"You'll have to fly from here in Miami to Boston, and then take another plane to Portland, where I've arranged for a limo to take you to the ferry dock for the crossing to the island. Your room is booked at the Sea Breeze hotel."

"I get sick on boats," Cohen said.

"That's the only way there. It's an island."

"Shit. What do I have for the rest of the day?"

"You have a meeting with the reporter from the *Washington Post.* It's about you know what," Monica said.

"Can't we put him off?"

"He already has sources from *The Lookingglass.* Former employees. He's going to print the story about your finances and the other things whether you talk on the record or not. It would be better if you told your side of the story."

"Maybe this trip to bum-fuck Maine will be good after all. It will give me a chance to unwind for at least a long weekend," Cohen said.

"Yes, make the best of it," Monica said.

26

Logan's fiancé Steve was the first to notice the drone hovering over the yacht he had rented for the pre-wedding dinner. The drone made several passes around the boat. At one point it dived nearly to the top of the boat's main mast. Logan had a good idea of where it came from. She bolted from her seat and went straight to her father.

"Dad, has Howard Cohen sent people here to spy on our wedding for his shitty tabloid?"

"I don't think Howard would do that," the senator said.

"Then how else would you explain the drone?" Logan said as she raised her middle finger skyward.

"Put your hand down. You'll just make things worse."

"Then it is from Howard."

"I'll have a chat with him when we get back to the hotel. Now enjoy the rest of the evening. Don't let this incident spoil things."

Senator Beasly sat down next to his girlfriend Heather, whose revealing dress attracted the attention of both the bridesmaids and the groomsmen. Their comments about her attire ranged from stunning to inappropriate, and about her personality from charming to slutty. After several strong drinks Heather took off her shoes and began gliding across the main deck, flirting with several of the men, including the senator's future son-in-law. The senator could see the fire in his daughter's eyes. He quickly said his goodbyes to the group and whisked his inebriated companion off of the boat and back to the Sea Breeze.

As Beasly walked into the hotel, he spotted Cohen at the bar.

"It must have been some party," Cohen said. "I've heard all about it already. I'm looking forward to seeing the footage later tonight."

"This wasn't what I had in mind when I invited you," Beasly said.

"Why don't you put that sumptuous woman barely standing next to you to bed and come back down and join me for a drink," Cohen said.

"Come on, Heather," Beasly said, pushing her toward the stairs.

Ten minutes later, Beasly returned and sat next to Cohen at the bar.

"Is sleeping beauty resting comfortably?" Cohen said.

"Fuck you, Howard."

"If it weren't for me, you wouldn't be getting that young piece of ass. Remember, I introduced you to her."

"For once, can't you just act like a normal person and leave my family in peace for the weekend?"

"You're one of the most recognizable senators in the country. And this is a grand social event. I have an obligation to my readers and viewers to cover the story. Freedom of the press and all of that bullshit."

"But please don't publish any pictures of Heather's behavior tonight."

"I warned you that she had a drinking problem," Cohen said. "But she has other skills that compensate for her indiscretions, I'm sure. But there is one thing that you can help me with."

"What's that?"

"I'm getting pressured by the IRS for nagging tax issues. The *Washington Post* is going to run a story on it in a matter of days. I'd like you to make a call to the IRS commissioner and tell him to back down."

"I can't do that, Howard. That would be political suicide for me."

"I know things about you that would make suicide an attractive option for you if they ever saw the light of day," Cohen said.

"Are you threatening a United States senator?"

"I don't have to make threats. I just have to make a few calls and Pandora's box will be wide open. I'm sure your Bible-quoting constituents would be interested in knowing how the former Sunday school teacher spent his time when his wife was dying from cancer. I'm sure the national press would be overjoyed to learn about the inside information I gave you about various stock deals. To keep those and other tidbits locked in my vault, all you have to do is make this tax case go away. I don't think that's too much to ask."

After Cohen finished his oration, Beasly pushed him off of his bar stool, sending him crashing to the floor. Beasly was about to kick him in the face when several patrons intervened. Cohen remained on the floor laughing while Beasly was restrained from further escalating the argument.

Cohen arose, thanking the strangers for interceding.

"I think the senator and I both have had too much to drink tonight," Cohen said. "I think I will retire. After all, tomorrow is a big day for the senator and his daughter. I wouldn't want to spoil that."

Beasly returned to his room shaken by his encounter with Cohen. To his surprise, Heather was awake when he opened the door. He told her about his conversation with Cohen.

"I have a plan that could get Cohen to back down from his threats. But I need your help," Beasly said.

Heather listened to the Beasly's plan. She agreed to help him.

The following morning dawned clear and bright. A perfect day for a wedding, Beasly thought as he put on his tuxedo. He hoped that the glorious celebration that was about to take place would distract everyone from the prior evening's unfortunate events. Logan looked stunning in her wedding dress. Successfully holding back his tears, Beasly escorted Logan down a flower-strewn path toward the water's edge where the ceremony would take place.

After the vows, the wedding party gathered under tents for the reception that began in the late afternoon and would continue through the evening. Steve and Logan had booked one of the most popular DJs from Washington to make the long trip to Moose Island to get the party started.

Propulsive dance music filled the air as darkness fell. Beasly looked at Heather, who once again was provocatively dressed but who had maintained her sobriety, under his instructions. Heather sauntered over to Cohen's table. Beasly saw them talking for a few minutes and then head toward the yacht, which Beasly had earlier checked to make sure that it was empty.

Less than fifteen minutes later, the sound of a woman's screams battled to be heard above the music. Beasly asked the DJ to turn the music down for a moment. The screams could be heard clearly now. The guests turned toward the boat. They saw Heather with her dressed ripped, exposing her breasts that were blood stained. She stumbled barefoot off of the boat toward the party tents.

Beasly was the first to meet her. He covered up her naked torso with his jacket. Now many people had gathered around them.

"What happened?" Beasly said.

"He's dead. He's dead," Heather said, sobbing and trying to catch her breath.

"Who's dead?"

"Cohen. Howard Cohen. He raped me and then I stabbed him. He's dead," Heather said as she collapsed to the ground.

Within seconds of those words coming from her mouth, multiple people dialed 911. The wedding celebration had ended.

27

Bleach blond, surgically-enhanced breasts, a beauty queen. The clichés multiplied in Nadine's head as she sat across from Heather Gilford the day after she admitted stabbing Howard Cohen in the chest. Heather's face still was bruised from the fight she put up trying to avoid being raped, according to her account.

"Walk me through what happened between you and Cohen from the time you talked to him at the wedding reception to the time of the assault on the boat," Nadine said.

"I had a few drinks. I admit that. But I was not drunk," Heather explained. "I had known Howard for many years. He helped get me into broadcasting. I went over the say hello and to catch up on things. He started talking about an opportunity at a national network. It was my chance to move up from the local station in Jackson. So, we continued talking and then I guess we starting walking around the grounds of the hotel. Then he suggested that we board the boat because it was growing colder. I had no reason to be fearful of Howard. He was like a father to me. I wasn't uncomfortable being alone with Howard."

"Then what happened after you went on the boat?"

"We went below deck and were sitting in the galley. He found some whiskey in a cabinet and poured us a drink. Then another. I then said I should be getting back to Lindsey, who was probably wondering where I was. When I tried to leave, Howard grabbed me. He tried to kiss me but I pulled back. Then he put one hand over my mouth and another between my legs. He's a strong man with large hands. I couldn't scream. He was suffocating me. He slapped me several times in the face and then he ripped my dress. Then he pulled my panties off and raped me on the floor of the galley."

"Where did you find the knife?"

"After he had finished, I slapped him hard across the face. He hit me back and I fell against a cabinet. I got up and saw that several knives had been knocked to the floor in the scuffle. I grabbed one and slashed at Howard. I think I cut his right arm. He tried to pull the knife from my hand, but I then stabbed him in the chest. He slumped to the floor. That's when I ran out of the boat and back to the wedding reception. You know the rest."

Heather's examination in a hospital in Portland had confirmed that she indeed had been sexually assaulted. But what nagged at Nadine was the fact that Cohen had no known history of sexual abuse of women, and certainly not of rape. Cohen was recently divorced from his wife of thirty years and had lost tens of millions in the settlement. But was the bitterness of that episode enough to turn him into a sexual predator, and at a wedding reception of all places? Something didn't smell right.

After returning to Moose Island, Nadine spoke with several wedding guests who had seen an altercation between Cohen and Beasly the night before Logan's wedding.

"Where did this fight take place?" Nadine said.

"Right here in the hotel bar," a man said. "My buddy Rich and I were having a few beers at a table in the corner when we saw one guy walk up and sit next to another at the bar. Rich told me that was Senator Beasly, whom I had never seen or met before. Anyway, I didn't think more about it until I heard swearing and then these two old dudes were going at each other. Rich and I ran over and pulled them apart."

"Did you hear what they were arguing about?"

"No, sorry. I just figured they had too much to drink and things got out of hand. They both left after that."

An argument between Cohen and Beasly, and then the following day Cohen rapes Beasly's girlfriend and ends up dead. Nadine needed to hear the senator's story. But she was prepared for a politician's slick responses and possible misdirection and obfuscation.

"How is your daughter handling things?" Nadine said.

"She was quite upset at the turn of events. She blamed me partially, I guess."

"Why is that?"

"She didn't like the tabloid business that Howard was in. She thought he was sleazy and didn't want me to invite him."

"Why did you?"

"I've known him for a long time. And he is one of my major campaign donors. Money grants access, Detective McAfee. It's just the way things are in politics."

"Then why did you get into a fight with him the night before Logan's wedding?"

"Nothing important. We just had too much to drink."

"Were you shocked that he would rape Heather?"

"Completely. Although I didn't condone how Howard made his billions, he was always a gentleman as far as I knew. What he did was completely out of character. I was shocked and saddened when Heather told me the disgusting details at the hospital," Beasly said.

"I'd appreciate it if you could stay on the island for a few more days until I complete my investigation," Nadine said.

"What's left to investigate?"

"I just want to be thorough. I would actually like to interview Heather again tomorrow. Just to make certain of a few details."

"Of course," Beasly said. As he returned to his room, he became increasingly nervous about what Heather might divulge if she was pressured by a detective who knew how to trip someone up on possible inconsistencies in a victim's story. He wasn't sure that Heather would remain calm in the face of a seasoned questioner. But he had already formulated a contingency plan. There was too much at stake to leave anything to chance.

***

"I did what you asked," Heather said. "It was fucking disgusting, but I did it. Now it's your turn to keep your end of the bargain. I want that primetime network position."

"I'll work on it. You know that I have high-level contacts in the industry," Beasly said. "Let's have a drink and celebrate. To your bright future and to my being rid of a man who knew too much."

An hour later, Beasly walked down to the hotel bar alone. He greeted several wedding guests who had remained on the island. He knew how to work a room. They all expressed their condolences and shock over what had occurred. But, nevertheless, the wedding had been beautiful, they agreed.

"Thank you," Beasly said. "The newlyweds Logan and Steve have already left for their honeymoon in the south of France. I'll need to win re-election to pay for it."

Beasly then made a point of telling everyone that he was going for a walk along the beach to get some fresh air. He looked at his watch. After exactly thirty minutes, he retuned to his room. One minute later, he ran downstairs and asked for someone to help him.

"Help! My girlfriend has drowned in the bathtub," he yelled with the perfect pitch of grief and shock.

28

"When I left her, she was alive," Beasly told Nadine. "We had a few drinks, but I didn't think she was incapacitated. You need to understand that Heather likes to drink. But I wouldn't say she was an alcoholic."

"Yet she was involved in two incidents in the past three days that involved heavy drinking. One resulted in a murder and the other in her own death," Nadine said.

"It's tragic, I know. It was a combination of the liquor and the stress. That seems clear to me."

"The medical examiner said that her blood alcohol level was three times the legal limit. Yet you left her in the room alone."

"She was awake when I left to get some fresh air," Beasly said.

Other than the fact that Heather had drowned, there was no other evidence of foul play that could implicate the senator. Nadine, however, couldn't help but think there was a connection between Heather's accidental bathtub downing and the murder of Howard Cohen. Senator Beasly was linked to both, but was never present when either his friend or lover had perished.

"I think he has some culpability in both incidents," Nadine told Captain Davies. "But there's nothing that I could charge him with."

"Then you have to close both investigations. We know what happened to Cohen. We know what happed to Gilford. There's nothing more we can do."

"But I think that a U.S. senator possibly orchestrated both," Nadine said.

"Can you prove it?"

"No."

"Then let's move on."

***

Three days after Nadine was told to end the investigations, an article appeared in the *Washington Post* revealing that Cohen was under investigation by the IRS at the time of his death.

"Listen to this, Grandma," Nadine said. "The article says that Cohen was diverting money from his media holdings to offshore accounts in Cyprus and the Cayman Islands. And that after he died, all of his personal records in a vault in Miami were destroyed because of a stipulation in his will. The article then quotes several current and former employees who said that the vault contained dirt on many celebrities and politicians. Cohen used that information to leverage favors."

"You think Cohen had compromising information on this Beasly guy?"

"I do. But now we'll never know," Nadine said.

"You didn't actually think you could bring down a senator, did you?"

"Since when did you become so cynical?"

"I'm old, but I can read. And I know people. I know who gets away with things and who pays the price. The senator falls into the former category."

***

"How does our fundraising look for this quarter?" Beasly asked his chief of staff Larry Bates.

"We're up twenty-five percent over last quarter. You're getting a lot of sympathy donations following Heather's death. People see that you're holding up well despite the appalling personal tragedies you have endured recently," Bates explained.

"It's good for people to feel sorry for you," Beasly joked.

"It can't hurt."

"Do you think it's too early to begin socializing in public?"

"Why do you ask?"

"I've been seeing a woman for the past month or so. But quietly. You know her. It's Sandra Overland."

"The oil industry lobbyist."

"One in the same."

"She's a stunner."

"I'd wait a few more weeks. At least until the state dinner at the White House. That will be a good time to show the world that you're ready to move on."

"That's right. I have to show strength. I have to soldier on. But I don't have to do it alone. After all, we all need relationships. They show that politicians are human."

"The voters will like that," Bates agreed.

PART 5: LITERARY LION

29

When Nadine received the call to join a state police response to an armed standoff with a fringe militia group, she never would have imagined that her ex-husband would be among those hold up in a remote cabin, charged with smuggling military-grade munitions into the state. A tactical unit had cordoned off the area around the cabin and had removed all nearby residents, which fortunately were few in such a desolate locale.

"Duke is in there," Captain Davies informed Nadine. "Can you reason with him?"

"He's not the man I once knew," Nadine said.

"You don't think he'd actually open fire on you, do you?"

"I can't be certain, but I'll try talking to him," Nadine said.

Nadine yelled toward the cabin, saying that she wanted to talk to Duke Granger.

"Nadine, is that you?" Duke yelled back from inside the cabin.

"We need to talk, Duke."

"I'm here with other patriots, defending our right to bear arms," Duke said. "Get the fuck out of here."

"You know I can't do that. I have an obligation to uphold the law, which you and your companions have violated."

"We don't recognize your laws."

"That's crazy talk, Duke. You're smarter than that."

"Leave, Nadine. I don't want you to be collateral damage," Duke yelled.

A shot rang out, striking the ground next to Nadine's feet. She hit the ground and crawled for cover back behind a police vehicle.

"We can't sit here forever," Captain Davies said. "I'm ordering the assault."

The assembled tactical unit fired tear gas through the cabin's windows. The people inside the cabin opened fire on the police. The firefight raged for less than ten minutes. Then the woods became silent.

"Don't go in there, Nadine," Captain Davies urged.

Nadine complied with his order. A few minutes later, Davies emerged from the cabin. All he had to do was shake his head, and Nadine knew that Duke was among the casualties.

Nadine decided not to attend Duke's funeral. Given the circumstances of his death, her past relationship with him, and her current law enforcement position, she didn't feel it would have been appropriate.

In her private moments, however, she mourned Duke's loss. Her grandmother Martha often told her that life was one long story that contained many chapters, not all of which had happy endings. This particular tale, Nadine thought, would fall into the tragic category. She wondered if she could have done more to help Duke, if she could have loved him more. Regret was an emotion that was strikingly human, she thought. Regret about what you might have achieved, or regret about what you could have changed. Such emotions haunt people their entire lives, Nadine concluded. What really was a life well-lived? Would anyone remember her after she was dead? Does her work really matter much?

These dark thoughts sloshed through Nadine's mind for weeks following the firefight with the militia. Nadine knew that she needed a fresh case to focus her mind outward. She needed to immerse herself in a new chapter in her life, and one that she could be proud of.

***

Wilbur Lovell, he of the bulbous head and thick black glasses, contemplated somberly that celebrations to honor him meant that he was coming to the end of his life, not just creatively but biologically. At seventy-eight, he had not published poetry of literary merit, in both his eyes and that of critics and academics, for at least thirty years. His name endured only in graduate literature programs and writing workshops where the new generation of poets lionized his stylish, patrician verse but who never wanted to emulates it themselves. "All they really want to become is the next rap star," Lovell once snarled. Lovell was a poet who everyone talked about, whose precious lines could be quoted by many, but whose style had mostly gone out of fashion.

Yet this once famous poet was having an unexpected renaissance from the most unlikely of occurrences. Three years ago, the Yale University Press published, to mild fanfare, the collected Lovell-Cardinal letters. Lovell had donated them to the library at Yale, which was his alma mater. Forty years ago, Lovell and the poet Elizabeth Cardinal initiated an epistolary affair that eventually turned into sexual one, which led to both of them divorcing their spouses at the time. Their letters were surprisingly (some would say shockingly) erotic, humorous, and loving. Lovell and Cardinal moved from Boston and New York respectively to Moose Island, where they lived unmarried for ten years and reared one child, a daughter named Ariel.

Both Lovell and Cardinal, she of the burning brown eyes and feverish sensuality, were prone to fits of mania. What contemporary psychiatry would call manic depression. Their unusual relationship and tempestuous private lives at first raised eyebrows on the small, close-knit community of Moose Island. But the odd couple mainly kept to themselves and respected their neighbors' privacy, as their neighbors respected theirs. Old-timers recall fondly memories of the young Ariel gathering wildflowers in the spring and creating bouquets for some of the women on the island.

Both poets created some of their best work while living in the bucolic, isolated setting. What outsiders didn't know was that during those ten years both Wilbur and a retinue of doctors in Boston tried to control Elizabeth's deteriorating mental state. Eventually, she succumbed to her demons and she deliberately drowned herself during a raging November nor'easter storm. After her death, Wilbur moved back to Boston, where he resumed teaching at Harvard. He eventually married his book editor, and they raised Ariel together.

Now, Wilbur and a gathering of his fans and former colleagues were about to descend on Moose Island to celebrate his lifetime achievements and the release of the film *Regretfully Yours,* a major Hollywood production that recreated the Lovell-Cardinal love affair with all of its tenderness and tragedies. The producer and the director of the film were going to screen it in Moose Island's small village hall to a select number of guests.

Aside from the film screening, there would also be the unveiling of *The Complete Poems of Wilbur Lovell*, whose publication Constance Lovell, Wilbur's second legal wife, had spearheaded as the ultimate tribute to her aging husband. These dual events were scheduled for the second week of August. Most of the rooms at the Sea Breeze hotel had been booked for the occasion.

Wilbur, Constance, and Ariel boarded the ferry for the crossing to Moose Island on a steamy afternoon after making the drive up from Boston. It had been thirty years since Wilbur had seen the craggy shoreline, pine forests, and stunning cliffs of the island. After checking into their rooms, Wilbur asked Constance and Ariel to walk with him. He wanted to show them the cottage where he had lived with Elizabeth so many years ago. Although Ariel had been born on the island, her childhood memories of the island had faded over time. She could not have navigated to the cottage where she spent the first five years of her life, but Wilbur had no problems reaching the destination of the cozy, handsome cottage.

"It's smaller than I imagined," Constance said.

"It was enough for us at the time," Wilbur said. "Ariel, your room was that window to the far right on the second floor. You can see the ocean from there."

"I wish I could remember, but I don't," Ariel said. She could see the disappointment in her father's eyes. This place meant so much to him.

"I hear that the movie producers recreated the cottage in detail on another island in Novia Scotia," Constance said.

"More's the pity," Wilbur said.

"Should we knock on the door?" Ariel said.

"No. No. Please don't do that," Wilbur said. "I don't want to bother the residents. And I want to remember it as it was, not as it might be now."

"Let's head back to the hotel," Constance said, sensing her husband's fatigue and melancholy. "It's been a long day."

***

While the Lovell family was strolling through the island's shady paths, Lisa Henry, professor of literature and women's studies at Smith College, had disembarked on the island. For the past year, under the veil of secrecy, she had been reviewing the private journals of Elizabeth Cardinal. Henry was about to publish a biography of Cardinal in which she would claim that Wilbur Lovell was a serious abuser and that he drove Cardinal to commit suicide, if her death was indeed a suicide. Based on Cardinal's journals, Henry believed there was enough circumstantial evidence to support that Lovell could have had a hand in her drowning by constantly berating her and suggesting that he and their daughter would be better off if she was dead. Could Lovell have murdered Cardinal at the ocean and claimed that she drowned herself? Henry believed that this could have occurred, since Cardinal left no suicide note. To gain maximum publicity for her provocative assertions, she and her publisher had agreed to post an excerpt of her biography online and conduct an interview with the *New York Times* to coincide with the Lovell celebration on Moose Island.

"I want to show the world that Wilbur Lovell is not this charming, congenial poet of rambles through the woods. But that he was a cruel, violent man who psychologically tortured a talented poet for a decade," Henry said in the interview. "He can't hide in the shadows of history any longer."

30

Even though more and more of his fellow writers and former students flocked to Moose Island to pay tribute to the great man of poetry, Wilbur Lovell grew increasingly anxious. He never felt confident about his place in the literary Pantheon. He always said that he was just a humble small-town scribe from Keene, New Hampshire. Part of him felt that he didn't deserve such attention, much less being portrayed on screen by a handsome Hollywood actor.

He let Constance and Ariel handle all of the logistics of the book release celebration and the movie premiere that were going to occur in two days. He needed to retreat from the madding crowd and re-explore the island that he once called home when he a younger, more vibrant man. Since the weather was amenable, he began to wander again the trails with which he had become so familiar forty years ago. The smells of the pines, the sounds of the birds, the power of the crashing waves for a moment took him back in time. But then the pain in his legs reminded him that he was an old man who could no longer conjure a decent couplet to save his life. He didn't even realize until he was actually there that his rambles had taken him to the place where Elizabeth's body had been found. He recalled that two local men had come to his cottage while he was working and told him that she was dead. He followed them to the shoreline and looked at her lifeless body. Her hair covered with sand. Her face bruised from hitting the rocks. He didn't know how to tell Ariel that her mother was gone. He couldn't remember after all of these years the exact words that he used. He just left the island to bury Elizabeth's body in the family's cemetery plot in the Berkshires of western Massachusetts. He had never returned to Moose Island until now.

Since his hearing and eyesight had deteriorated over time as yet more reminders of the indignity of age, he hadn't noticed or heard that someone had been following him on his walking tour. After looking out to sea silently, he rose slowly to return to the hotel when he spotted a woman standing above him on an outcropping of rock.

"A beautiful day, isn't it?" she said.

"That it is," Wilbur said. The woman above him was hunched over. Her gray hair was tied back with a bandana. Her face was creased with deep wrinkles. But in spite of her age, there was a luminous sparkle in her eyes that startled Wilbur. Suddenly, he felt nervous, but was not sure why.

"You don't remember me, do you Wilbur?"

"I'm sorry, but I don't. Should I?"

"I'm Irene Michaud. But you knew me as Irene Miller when you were living on the island."

"That was a long time ago," Wilbur said. "I'm sorry but I didn't recognize you at first. You can't still be living here."

"Yes, I am. I only left the island for a brief time because of the incident. You know what I'm talking about, Wilbur."

Wilbur knew exactly what Irene was talking about. But he didn't want to relive that time. He tried to move past her. But she grabbed him by the arm. The strength of her grip startled him. There was anger in her hands, he thought.

"Neither one of us can repair the past. I've moved on. You must have moved on, too. You said your surname was Michaud. You must have married and had a family," Wilbur said.

"My husband is dead and I could never have any children after the incident in Boston."

"I didn't know it would turn out that way for you."

"You ruined my life when you were here on the island. After all of these years I tried to forget, but I couldn't. I occasionally read about you in the papers, like when you won those literary prizes and were invited to the White House. I thought to myself: what if people really knew what kind of a man you really were? Does your new wife and daughter know about this chapter in your past? I can tell by the way you averted your gaze that they don't. Now with all of these people here ready to praise you to high heaven, maybe I'll just crash the party."

"Leave them alone. They don't know about you. What would be the point after all of this time? If you said something, you wouldn't be hurting me. I'm an old man. You can't hurt me now," Wilbur said.

"Maybe you are not the person I want to suffer. I've been waiting for you to arrive since the announcement was made about this grand celebration. And, my goodness, there's been a movie made about your loving relationship with Elizabeth. Who's going to portray me in the film? Oh, nobody. Because in the end, I was a nobody to you. But yet: here I am, standing right in front of you with these same eyes that inspired you to write many of your precious poems," Irene said.

"Now you are just mocking me," Wilbur said. "I have to go. I can tell that my arrival here had stirred up waves of bitterness inside of you. I can't tell you how to feel. All I can ask is that you just leave me alone. I'll be off the island soon enough."

"You were always dismissive of me. I was young then. Too much in awe of you, the older man. But I can see that you're nothing special, in spite of all of the hoopla surrounding you now. You've earned a lot of accolades over the decades. But you know what: you've never really paid a price for anything," Irene said. "Maybe that time has come."

"What do you mean?" Wilbur said.

"Don't you need to get back to your family?" Irene reminded him sarcastically.

Wilbur walked back to the hotel as briskly as his old legs could take him. Before going back to his room, he stopped to have a whiskey at the bar. But his hands remained shaking. Constance could not see him like this. He waited until he had regained a measure of equilibrium. He finally opened the door to his hotel room. Constance greeted him with a smile.

"How was your walk?" she said.

"It brought back a lot of memories," Wilbur said.

31

Irene returned to her small house in a secluded area of the island where she used to live with her husband Arlen Michaud until his death from cancer five years ago. Arlen worked for the island's power station and was known as a congenial, reliable handyman for any needed household repairs. Irene had met him while she was working one summer as a waitress at the Seas Breeze hotel. She was only seventeen years old when she arrived on the island for what she thought would be a summer job. But she never left Moose Island. She continued to waitress at the hotel until she developed severe back pain. She now survived on Arlen's pension and Medicaid payments.

It was shortly after marrying Arlen that she informed him that she could not have children. She only revealed that she had an issue with her womb. Arlen was against adoption; he didn't want to deal with any social or genetic baggage from an anonymous family. So, the couple settled in to living a childless life together for twenty-five years. Outwardly, they appeared content with the arrangement. But Irene burned with anger over what had happened between her and Wilbur Lovell the year before she met and married Arlen.

Irene brought out photos of herself when she first arrived on the island from a small Maine village near the border with Quebec. It was her chance to feel some independence. It was only a week after her arrival that she heard whispers about the eccentric poet and his lover who lived on the island. She had never heard of Wilbur Lovell. But then one day she met him while she was swimming alone in the ocean, a divine luxury that she had always dreamed about. Before arriving at Moose Island, she had never seen the ocean. Standing there above her on the rocks holding her towel was a tall man with curly brown hair and wearing glasses with black frames. He stood rigid like an oak tree, smiling broadly. She remembered the first conversation that they had:

"You swim like a nymph."

"A what?" Irene replied.

"It's a mythical female creature, like a mermaid."

"That's a compliment, I guess."

"Indeed, it is. What's your name?"

"Irene. Irene Miller."

"I'm Wilbur Lovell."

"I've heard of you. You're a writer or something like that."

"A poet, to be specific," Wilbur said. "Here's your towel."

From that magical and unexpected encounter, Wilbur and Irene began meeting secretly during her first summer on the island. Together, they found a small abandoned cottage where they had their liaisons. The same cottage that's now inhabited by the artist Wendy Wiseman, Irene thought to herself. If only Wendy knew what went on there so many years ago.

Irene knew that Wilbur went home each night to Elizabeth and their young daughter Ariel. He told Irene, however, they he and Elizabeth had an understanding about their unusual arrangement. Consumed by jealously and curiosity, Irene sometimes secretly walked to the house in which Wilbur lived. Sometimes she saw Wilbur chasing Ariel around the yard. Sometimes he heard him violently berating Elizabeth in the most vile and unflattering terms.

When Irene heard such things, she couldn't believe they came from the same man that she had come to know.

By August of that first summer on the island, Irene knew that she was pregnant. In her small-town innocent way, she thought that Wilbur would leave Elizabeth and begin a new life with her. He often told her that he would. Instead, he exploded with anger, slapping her hard across the face and sending her crumbling to the ground. He then demanded that she accompany him to Boston, where someone he knew would take care of her "situation," as he referred to it. That someone botched the procedure, leaving her fighting for her life. She then learned from another doctor that she would never have children again because of what the other man, whom the doctor called a "butcher," had done.

She never told her family what she had endured. Only that she would not be returning home. She planned to stay and work on the island. She wanted Wilbur to see her every day. She wanted to torture him with her continued presence. But that autumn was when Elizabeth drowned and Wilbur departed the island, never to return. Until now.

Irene looked again at the young woman in the photo with the long legs, upright frame, and sparkling eyes. She found it hard to believe that she was looking at herself. It had grown late. The time was nearly midnight. Irene decided to take a secluded path that only a local would know to the village hall, where the movie premiere was planned for the following night. She looked at the promotional poster that had been placed next to the entrance. The actor who played the young Wilbur Lovell was handsome she thought, but he didn't have the intensity in his eyes that Wilbur once had. No actor could pull that off, she decided.

She surveyed the area once more before she went to the back of the hall and started the fire. She waited until the flames began creeping up the wooden siding and then to the roof line. She knew that the building would be fully engulfed in a matter of minutes. She retreated quickly to her house.

***

"Who would do a thing like torch the village hall?" Constance said the following morning after the fire had been extinguished by the island's volunteer fire crew. "There's no place else on the island where the producer can show the film."

"Maybe it's for the best," Wilbur mused. "I would have felt uncomfortable sitting there anyway."

"Come now," Constance chided him. "You would have loved it. Anyway, the producer said that he would put the movie online for a special digital preview so that guests can watch it on their computers. So, not all was lost. Thanks to the wonders of modern technology. And we still have the book launch gala tomorrow evening."

Wilbur suspected who the arsonist was. He didn't say a word to anyone, however. Irene's words about him paying the price buzzed in his head.

32

Before the evening's book launch and author signing, Constance had arranged for a group of scholars to hold a public seminar about Wilbur's work and life. One of the scholars who had been invited was Lisa Henry, who early in her career wrote several well-received academic articles on the influence of the British Lake District poets on Wilbur's creative development. The rumor was that she had been working on an important book on Wilbur and Elizabeth, but no one knew for sure what it was about. Henry and her publisher had kept the details of the work secret. But now Henry was there in front of over one hundred people. The room buzzed when she took her place behind the podium to commence her presentation.

For the next hour, Henry laid out in stark details, using lengthy passages from Elizabeth Cardinal's diary, of Wilbur's physical, sexual, and emotional abuse of Elizabeth during the decade that they lived on Moose Island. The assembled crowd gasped when Henry slowly read one passage written shortly after Elizabeth had given birth to Ariel in which Wilbur forced her to have painful sex with him. In other diary entries, Elizabeth chronicled her fear that Wilbur would one day kill her in a rage. The diary also revealed, Henry continued, that Wilbur had a lover while living on the island. Elizabeth never revealed the lover's identity, only referring to her as the "nubile water nymph."

When Henry concluded her presentation, a few scholars rose in Wilbur's defense, noting that Elizabeth had a manic-depressive personality and that the diary could have been pure fiction. Henry defended her thesis, noting that she interviewed Elizabeth's friends and family members who were still alive to verify the accounts in the diary.

"There is no doubt in my mind," Henry said confidently, "that Wilbur Lovell abused Elizabeth Cardinal relentlessly, driving her eventually to suicide. Although, let me say for the record that I think it is equally plausible, given Elizabeth's fear, that Wilbur might have killed her and that he lied about the circumstances surrounding her death."

"Liar! Liar!" Ariel Lovell screamed from the back of the Sea Breeze's dining room where the presentation was being held. "You weren't there. I was. I never saw my father hurt my mother. There was only love between them. Yes, I saw my mother have what she called 'moods,' but my father tried to help her as much as he could. He encouraged her. But ultimately the demons inside of her won out. I'm just glad my father is not here to witness this garbage. He had the good sense to stay away this afternoon."

"I understand your feelings, Ms. Lovell," Henry retorted. "But you were a child when these events occurred, mostly out of your sight. You could not have possibly understood the dynamics of their relationship at that age."

Before the battle between the scholar and daughter escalated into something truly nasty, Constance shut down the seminar, thanked everyone for attending, and reminded them of the book signing after dinner that evening.

As the attendees slowly drifted out of the dining hall, several of the scholars could be heard speculating about who the secret lover was. Was she still alive? Could she be found and interviewed? Would she reveal herself? And why didn't Lovell himself attend the seminar?

Constance guided Ariel out of the room and into the August sunshine. The ocean glimmered in the distance. Sailboats plied the straight between the island and the mainland. Their sails looking like shark fins.

"Where is your father?" Constance said.

"I haven't seen him since breakfast this morning. He told me that he just wanted time alone. He seemed particularly upset about the fire at the village hall," Ariel said. "You know the moods he can get himself into. I bet he's just been sitting alone somewhere on the island."

"If he's not back by dinner, we have to look for him."

"I'm sure he'll return by then."

***

Since she arrived on the island, Wendy Wiseman liked to spend glorious afternoons wandering the least travelled portions of the island, hideaways to which the tourists never ventured. This day, she ventured to a secluded cove with her art materials. She intended to work on a new canvas while imbibing the warm sea air. As she descended a steep, precarious path she noticed a body lying in the rocks. She moved closer, finding an older man lying motionless. His head was bloodied. Upon closer inspection, she noticed that his pants had been pulled down. His genitals had been mutilated. She didn't bother screaming. No one would have heard her anyway. She pulled out her cell phone, but she could not get a signal on that remote side of the island. She scrambled back up the path until she could get cell reception.

***

"Grandma, I have to go to Moose Island for a while," Nadine said. "There's been a report of a murder there."

"Who?"

"Not sure. But we have to bring in a mountain rescue team to recover the body. I'm meeting them at Stillwater Cove to make the last ferry of the day," Nadine said.

When Nadine arrived at the ferry dock, the rescue team and forensics professionals were waiting for her. They crossed over to the island together and met Wendy

Wiseman, who directed them to the site where she had discovered the body.

Daylight was fading by the time the team arrived at the steep trail that led down to the rocky shore. After more than an hour, the body had finally been retrieved.

"My god," Nadine said, while shining a flashlight on the mutilated corpse. "Do we have an ID?"

"Here's his wallet," said a member of the forensics team.

"Wilbur Lovell," Nadine said. "Have you ever seen him before?"

"No," Wendy said. "But since I made the 911 call, I found out that he's an author. There was a big celebration being planned tonight in his honor at the Sea Breeze hotel."

"Did you find any weapon down there?" Nadine asked the team.

"Nothing. But my guess is that he was killed by a sharp blow to the back of the head by a heavy rock. Then when he was either unconscious or already dead, his genitals were mutilated, causing severe blood loss. The medical examiner will have to determine the exact cause of death."

"We need to get this body off of the island tonight," Nadine said. "I'll make a call to the Coast Guard to send a boat to take you and the victim off of the island. But first I need to find his family to identify him."

The team took the body to the dock to await pick up. Nadine headed to the Sea Breeze hotel. Before she could get there, she received a call from Captain Davies.

"Where are you right now?" he said.

"I've just recovered the victim's body and I'm searching for his family," Nadine explained.

"Get to the hotel immediately. There's been an attack on a woman. And another person has been reported missing," Davies said.

"Fuck" Nadine said. "What is happening here?"

"Get moving and find out."

Nadine ran up the hill from the dock to the hotel, where dozens of people were milling about the dining room. Nadine noticed a tall pyramid of books stacked in the corner of the room next to a picture of the man whom she knew was dead.

A small group of people surrounded a woman who sat in a chair with a glass of water in front of her. Her breathing was labored and she looked frightened.

"Please step aside," she ordered. "I'm Detective Nadine McAfee. What just happened here?" Who are you?"

"I'm Professor Lisa Henry. I was attacked outside of my room when I was coming down for dinner. Someone tried to strangle me. I fought her off and she ran away."

"You said 'her.' Did you recognize who did this?"

"Yes. Ariel Lovell. She tried to kill me."

"Is she any relation to Wilbur Lovell?"

"Yes. His daughter," a woman said, stepping forward. "I'm her stepmother Constance Lovell."

"Where is she now?"

"I don't know. I can't find her or my husband, who has been missing since this morning. He was supposed to be here for this celebration."

"Mrs. Lovell, I'm sorry to inform you that your husband has been found dead. He's been murdered."

Constance screamed. She was held up by several people in the crowd that had encircled her.

"Come with me, Mrs. Lovell."

"We need to find Ariel," Constance repeated over and over before then saying: "I want to see Wilbur."

"We will find her," Nadine said. "But now I need you to come with me to the dock. Your husband's body is there."

Nadine steadied Constance as they walked to the dock. She did not want to reveal the gruesome details of her husband's death. But she did need Constance to identify the body. Constance wept when she saw her husband lying there, his eyes cold and blank like black marbles.

Nadine called Captain Davies. "I need several officers sent here immediately. There's a woman missing. The male victim's daughter. I don't want to find her dead also."

It would be a long night, Nadine thought. A full moon had arisen. Its yellow light danced on the calm sea and illuminated the body bag containing Wilbur Lovell, the great poet of nature at its most sublime.

33

The keen tactical advantage that Nadine and her now assembled search team had was the fact that their suspect was on an island. Unless the killer had access to a boat, Nadine thought, the person who murdered Wilbur Lovell and had likely kidnapped Ariel was somewhere on this island that was only ten miles long and three miles wide.

The word went out quickly among the residents to shelter at home but to report any suspicious activity on their property. Nadine led a group of two officers toward the north end of the island, while two other officers scoured the south end. The plan was for each group to move inland toward the center of the island. Meanwhile, the Coast

Guard circled the island searching for any bodies in the water or that may have washed up on shore. Nadine hoped that such a worst-case scenario would not materialize.

The north end of Moose Island contained few residents and a dense forest. Nadine recalled being in this area when she first met the Druid-loving artist Wendy Wiseman. Memories of this area returned to Nadine. She told the other two officers to follow her. When they arrived at Wendy's cottage, Nadine ordered the officers to have their weapons drawn.

Nadine called out to see if Wendy had returned to her home. There was no answer. She moved toward the door and pushed it open. Lying on the floor with a stab wound to the chest was Wendy, who was still breathing but bleeding profusely. Her shirt was stained crimson.

Nadine radioed to a medical crew that was standing by at the ferry dock. She gave them directions to the cottage and informed them of the nature of the Wendy's wounds.

"Wendy," Nadine said. "Medical personnel are on their way. Can you talk? Who did this to you?"

"Irene. Irene Michaud. After I met you at the dock, I returned here and found Irene standing in my studio with another woman. Before I could ask a question or understand what was taking place, Irene lunged at me with a knife. Then she and the other woman fled to the east, toward the cliffs," Wendy said.

"Thanks. That's very useful information," Nadine said. "Officer Williams will stay here with you until the EMTs arrive. Just hang on."

Nadine motioned the other officer to follow her toward the cliffs. She hoped that she wouldn't be too late to prevent another tragedy.

***

"Why are we stopping here?" Ariel said. Irene had brought her to the precipice of a cliff that plunged two hundred feet to the Atlantic below. She stood close to Ariel. Her knife poised to slash Ariel's throat. "Why are you doing this?"

"You have no idea who I am, do you?" Irene said.

"I just know you are some crazy woman. You stabbed that lady for no reason."

"Oh, Ariel, I'm not crazy. I know exactly what I'm doing. I never thought I would ever get the chance, however. I'm getting my revenge on the people who hurt me long ago."

"How could I have hurt you? I don't even know you."

"We met once, briefly, when you were just a little girl living on this island. Your father introduced us once in secret at that very cottage when I stabbed that woman, who never should have moved here. That cottage was once a special place to your father and me. But your father betrayed me, and that's why he had to be killed."

"What do you mean? Why did you say my father was killed?"

"You must have fled the hotel before the news had gotten to you. Wilbur Lovell is dead. And I killed him."

"But why? Why?" Ariel sobbed. "I don't understand."

"He ruined my life. I was his lover all of those years ago. I became pregnant. But he took me to a butcher in Boston, who ruined my chances of ever having children again. Your father was selfish and cruel, not only towards me but to your mother."

"My mother wasn't well. Dad tried to help her as best he could."

"You really think that your mother killed herself during a storm?"

"Yes, of course."

"I was there that November night. I regularly spied on your family from the woods that surrounded your house. The night of the storm, your mother ran outside after having, I assume, some altercation with your father. Wilbur soon followed her. Even in the pounding rain, Wilbur pursued Elizabeth down to the ocean. I followed both of them. Their argument continued. The wind was so strong and the waves were so furious that I could not hear what they were yelling at each other. All I saw was that Wilbur pulled Elizabeth by the hair, dragging her into the surf. She struggled to return to shore. But Wilbur held her down amidst the storm's fury. Drenched and fighting against the storm-driven waves, he made it back safely. He never looked back as your mother's body disappeared under the water."

"I don't believe you!" Ariel screamed. "And even if what you're saying happened and you witnessed it, why didn't you report this to the police?"

"Because I loved him. I saw her death as my chance to finally be with him. To help raise you. To be a mother to you. But he abruptly left the island and never returned," Irene said. "Now, I want to erase everything from that time, everything that Wilbur Lovell ever touched. Including you."

Irene then heard a noise coming from the woods to the west. Nadine and another officer emerged from the forest, their weapons pointed at her.

"Let her go, Irene," Nadine ordered.

"How do you know my name?"

"Wendy told me. She's still alive. Let Ariel go. There's no reason to harm her."

Irene maneuvered herself behind Ariel so that neither Nadine nor the other officer could shoot her without hitting Ariel.

"I have plenty of reasons, which Ariel herself now knows," Irene said. "Don't come any closer."

Nadine was too far away from Irene and Ariel to consider rushing at them. Irene would have the time and the space to slash Ariel's throat.

"Let her go. You obviously have some long-held grievance with the Lovell family. If you want people to know about it, if you want to explain your side of the story, you have to let Ariel go," Nadine said.

"No matter what I say, there will always be those who put Wilbur Lovell on a pedestal. Yes, he was brilliant. Yes, he wrote beautiful poetry, some of which he wrote for me and about me. But he wasn't a good man. What I have to say will never matter. I was a nobody then, and I am still a nobody. And when you're just an innocent girl from the backwoods of Maine, no one cares that you're alive. And no one will care that I'm gone," Irene said before stopping and gazing down at the ocean below. "I always loved the ocean from the first time I arrived here. I loved to swim. I want to return to the water."

Irene then deliberately fell backwards while still holding Ariel. Both women disappeared over the edge of the cliff. Nadine rushed forward in time to see the pair, now separated in the air, hit the surf far below. Nadine contacted the Coast Guard to begin searching for the bodies, but she was certain that neither woman survived.

***

Two hours later, the lifeless bodies of Irene and Ariel arrived at the ferry dock. Constance Lovell had to be taken back to her hotel room and sedated after seeing the dead body of her step- daughter so soon after identifying the body of her husband.

Inside of the Sea Breeze hotel, the guests who had gathered to celebrate the life and work of Wilbur Lovell grabbed their free copy of his collected poems and organized an impromptu poetry reading in his memory. Notably absent was Lisa Henry, who had quietly departed the island, pleased that her agent had booked appearances for her on three network morning programs.

Before departing Moose Island to return to the mainland and write her report for Captain Davies, Nadine also picked up a copy of Lovell's poems that someone had discarded on the ferry to Stillwater Cove. The jacket cover featured two photos: one of Lovell as an old man and the other as a dashing younger man. Nadine could see why he could seduce women such as Elizabeth and Irene.

Nadine flipped through the poetry volume that she intended to give to her grandmother, who loved to read. Nadine came across a poem about a woman who glided through the water like a dolphin and who lured men to the water's edge where she killed them. Nadine had once heard that the greatest creative minds had an uncanny sense of their own destiny. She wondered if Wilbur Lovell had ever contemplated that his violent death would cement his place as a literary lion who would not be forgotten.

Nadine gently placed the poetry volume on the passenger seat of her car that was parked at the dock in Stillwater Cove. All that remained of the old man was his words, she thought as she drove home. She didn't know exactly why, but she felt an obligation to safeguard that thick volume that contained both the darkest thoughts and the deepest emotions of a fellow human being who no longer would be seen or heard by those who loved him.